Also by E. D. Baker

Power of a PRINCESS

A **More Than a Princess** NOVEL

E. D. BAKER

BLOOMSBURY
CHILDREN'S BOOKS
NEW YORK LONDON OXFORD NEW DELHI SYDNEY

BLOOMSBURY CHILDREN'S BOOKS
Bloomsbury Publishing Inc., part of Bloomsbury Publishing Plc
1385 Broadway, New York, NY 10018

BLOOMSBURY, BLOOMSBURY CHILDREN'S BOOKS, and the Diana logo
are trademarks of Bloomsbury Publishing Plc

First published in the United States of America in November 2019
by Bloomsbury Children's Books

Bloomsbury books may be purchased for business or promotional use. For information
on bulk purchases please contact Macmillan Corporate and Premium Sales Department at
specialmarkets@macmillan.com

Library of Congress Cataloging-in-Publication Data
Names: Baker, E. D., author.
Title: Power of a princess / by E.D. Baker.
Description: New York : Bloomsbury, 2019.
Summary: Aislin, with a carefully chosen group of girls who are brave and loyal
but not typical companions for a princess, sets out to restore balance and
peace among magical creatures.
Identifiers: LCCN 2019004272 (print) | LCCN 2019006473 (e-book)
ISBN 978-1-68119-769-2 (hardcover) • ISBN 978-1-68119-772-2 (e-book)
Subjects: | CYAC: Fairy tales. | Princesses—Fiction. | Magic—Fiction. | Fairies—Fiction. |
Imaginary creatures—Fiction.
Classification: LCC PZ8.B173 Pow 2019 (print) | LCC PZ8.B173 (e-book) | DDC [Fic]—dc23
LC record available at https://lccn.loc.gov/2019004272

Book design by Danielle Ceccolini
Typeset by Westchester Publishing Services
Printed and bound in the U.S.A. by Berryville Graphics Inc., Berryville, Virginia
2 4 6 8 10 9 7 5 3 1

To find out more about our authors and books visit www.bloomsbury.com and sign up
for our newsletters.

I DEDICATE THIS BOOK TO KIM, ELLIE, AND
KEVIN FOR BEING THERE WHEN I NEEDED YOU,
TO VICTORIA WELLS ARMS AND ALLISON MOORE
FOR YOUR QUESTIONS AND SUGGESTIONS,
AND TO ALL MY SUPER FANS WHOSE
ENTHUSIASM MEANS SO MUCH TO ME.

Chapter 1

AISLIN DUCKED INTO THE cave opening and let her eyes adjust to the dim light. Small, furry creatures scurried out of sight, and the snake that had been hunting them glanced at her before slipping into a crevice. A gentle breeze wafted past her out of the cave opening, fluttering the spiders' webs that blocked her path. "This is a breathing mountain," Aislin murmured to herself. There must be other openings to the outside that allowed the air to flow in and out.

Using the stick she'd brought with her, Aislin knocked down the webs, clearing a path. Although she might have walked into the webs that she couldn't see in the bright sunlight, her eyes were keener when the light was weaker. She could see perfectly well in the near-absolute dark—an attribute of her pedrasi relatives.

Aislin closed her eyes and used her pedrasi senses to learn what was around her. Just past the rocky outcropping, a passage led farther into the mountain. Although an opening to her left led to a large cave, Aislin could sense that it was a dead end. She opened her eyes and took a few more steps to where the walls were farther apart and the ceiling was higher.

Aislin reached into her pocket and took out the fairy light that her friend Poppy had crafted for her. It was about the size of an apple and gave off a warm glow. It wasn't much, but it was all Aislin needed to see clearly in even the biggest, darkest caverns where no light penetrated from the outside. As a pedrasi, she could navigate through a dark cave using her other senses, of course, but Aislin liked to see the cave walls as well, enjoying the beauty she often found.

It was especially important now that she was exploring Mount Gora for her grandfather.

As Aislin walked around the outcropping, she thought about what her pedrasi grandfather, King Talus, had said when he asked her to help update the map of Mount Gora, the northernmost mountain in the range. "No pedrasi has lived there since before my father was king. Mountains change and evolve, albeit slowly. Rocks fall, rivers change their courses, the features in the caverns grow.

"While you're there, learn what you can do with your newfound abilities. Test yourself. No one lives in the cave now, so you won't hurt anyone if your magic does something...unexpected."

Aislin thought briefly of the escort waiting for her at the base of the mountain. As steady as the rock around her, the guards would wait there whether her mission took three hours, three days, or three years. Aislin hoped it wouldn't take much time at all. She didn't have a lot of food with her, for one thing— just some hardtack, a pouch of dried berries, and a hollowed-out gourd filled with water, all tucked into the knapsack she had slung over her shoulder.

She also had to think about Twinket. The living doll had insisted on coming with her to the mountain, even though King Talus had commanded that no one could enter the cave with Aislin. But Twinket was one of Aislin's closest friends. A long-ago gift from Aislin's fairy grandmother, Queen Surinen, she had many wonderful qualities, but patience was not one of them. If Aislin took more than a day, Twinket would never stop complaining about how long she'd had to wait.

Ducking under the jagged rock that partially barred the entrance to the passageway, Aislin had to walk another ten feet before she could stand upright again. The only illumination now was that of the fairy light that floated in front of her, but it was more than enough. The rock was dry, though she could sense water up ahead. Long and narrow, this was little more than a tunnel that led into a maze of other passageways.

The maze was convoluted enough to get a non-pedrasi lost and disoriented. For a pedrasi, the way was as plain as if it were marked with road signs. Aislin would have loved to explore the level, but there were so many things in this mountain calling to her that it would be a waste of her time to spend too long on one.

Closing her eyes again, she used her senses to link her to the mountain. Aislin *felt* all the passageways spread out before her, well enough that she could walk them with her eyes shut, so well that she would always remember them and be able to draw on them even years from now. Letting her senses reach out, she felt where angles led up and down, some walled off with fallen rock, others leading to open shafts where a misstep would be very, very bad. When she found a few that were safe, she let her senses go up to the next level where her mind sparked with interest. There was something there that she had to see for herself; it was definitely a cavern where she'd want to use her eyes as well as her other senses.

Aislin strode along the path she'd chosen, ducking where she sensed she might hit her head as she picked her way across the uneven floor. She found the passage that angled upward and walked faster, eager with anticipation. Her grandparents had told her about places like the cavern ahead, but she'd never seen one before.

A salamander skittered past. A bat narrowly missed bumping into her. A pale cricket hopped out of her way. She was always amazed at how many creatures lived in the absolute dark of the caves. It was chilly here, too, though nothing that a pedrasi couldn't handle; their extra layer of fat kept them comfortable underground, where it stayed close to fifty-four degrees.

When she reached a part of the tunnel that was riddled with crevices and small openings, Aislin had the strongest feeling that someone was watching her. She looked around, but didn't see anyone, so she assumed it was merely a bat or salamander. The passage grew steeper, with the angle becoming so abrupt that Aislin had to find hand- and footholds. When the floor suddenly leveled out, she stood and looked around. The cavern was one of the most beautiful things she'd ever seen. White stalactites hung from the ceiling, reaching toward the stalagmites down below. Ribbon rock rippled along sections of the wall. Crystals grew everywhere, glittering in the glow of the fairy light.

I wish Tomas could see this, she thought, recalling the human boy she had met in Morain. When King Tyburr held both of them in his castle, Tomas had become more than just another captive. He had become her friend.

Aislin was careful not to touch any of the crystals that grew on the floor as she picked her way to a flat spot that looked as if it had been made into a seat. Setting her knapsack on the ground, she sat down beside it to gaze at the cave around her. The crystals were even more extraordinary than she'd first thought. Although they were all gorgeous, she particularly liked the ones that grew in the shapes of delicate flowers.

Feeling the urge to play, Aislin reached out with her mind to shape some of the rougher crystals into her own flowers and spell out her name, then those of her grandparents, King Talus and Queen Amethyst.

After a while, Aislin recalled why she was there. She closed her eyes so the beautiful crystals wouldn't distract her, and tapped back into her pedrasi senses. Without leaving her seat, she explored the cavern and the rest of that level in the mountain, noting features that she'd have to include on her map. She knew she might be faster and more adept at exploring if she was stronger, so she reached into the rock and drew power until her hair crackled with energy and she could feel the blood coursing through her veins.

She searched the mountain above her, noting the warren of caves that had housed the pedrasi who had once lived there. Along with great halls for meetings, there were smaller caves for families, caves with vents for cooking, and deep shafts for disposing of trash. A larger cave just below the mountain peak boasted a throne made of stone. Aislin decided that the rooms around it must have been where her ancestors had lived and held court.

Aislin was still in tune with the mountain when she heard knocking. When she opened her eyes, she was surprised to find that her fairy light was gone, as was the knapsack she'd brought with her. The knocking came again, and she tilted her head to listen. Although she couldn't see them, she sensed that four beings were crowded behind the column just ahead.

When she heard rustling, as if they were about to run, she got to her feet. Walking toward the other side of the column, she called out in her commanding voice, "Stay where you are!" The rustling stopped. Although there wasn't even a tiny ray of light in the cavern, she sensed where they were and looked directly at them, asking, "What are you doing here?"

They all responded at once. "We want to know why you're here."

"How did you find us in the dark?"

"Why am I stuck here?"

"Who are you?"

Aislin sighed and said, "Give me back my possessions and I'll tell you."

"What makes you think we took them?"

"No one else is here," said Aislin. "Please hand them over."

The one holding her knapsack grumbled as he handed it to her, while another reached into a large leather sack and took out the fairy light. As the light floated back to the princess, stopping to hover above her head, she took a good look at the little thieves and realized that they were spriggans. They varied in height by a few inches, though none of them were over a foot and a half tall. Three were male and one was female, and they all had coarse hair that stood up around their heads. Their skin, hair, and miners' clothes were completely gray. Familiar with the spriggans who lived with the pedrasi in Deephold, Aislin knew this was because of the stone dust that covered them.

"I didn't know that any spriggins lived here," she told them. "My grandfather thinks Mount Gora is uninhabited."

"We've lived here forever," one replied. "I've heard that we were supposed to leave when the pedrasi did, but we fooled them and stayed behind."

Curious, Aislin said, "I know that spriggans like to play tricks, but I didn't think your people stole from pedrasi. Why did you take my things?"

The spriggan who had taken her knapsack looked surprised. "You're pedrasi? You don't look like it." He was shorter than the others and had very large ears. "Plus, you were sitting there with your eyes closed and didn't seem to notice when we knocked on the stone."

A female spriggan in a softer voice chimed in. "We were going to take your shoes next, but then your hair sparked and you began to glow. We hid so we could watch you, then you found us anyway. What are you? You don't look like a fairy, but that light must be magic. Are you a magic user? Did you make that light yourself?"

Aislin pulled her knapsack onto her shoulder and glanced at the fairy light floating above her head. "A fairy friend made that light and yes, it is magic. I'm half fairy and half pedrasi. My name is Aislin and I'm the granddaughter of King Talus."

"Who is King Talus?" the tallest spriggan asked.

"The king of the pedrasi. His father was King Anthracite and his grandfather was King Obsidian."

"My father's father's father's father was a personal friend of King Obsidian's!" piped up the female spriggan. "If you're the king's granddaughter, that means you're a pedrasi princess! My name is Kimble, by the way, and these goofuses are Jinxie, Borry, and Smax."

"I am a princess," Aislin said. "My mother is Queen Maylin and—"

Suddenly she felt a disturbance somewhere below her. She stopped talking abruptly to focus on what she was sensing.

"What's wrong?" asked Kimble. "You just got a funny look on your face."

"Something is going on in a lower level. I think someone—or something—is down there."

The spriggans glanced at each other and nodded knowingly. "The trolls must be back," Kimble told her. "They carry torches and snoop around breaking stuff. Lately they've been going to the lower levels. We don't know what they're doing because we stopped going down there a couple of years ago."

"Why?" asked Aislin.

"Because of Old Grumpy," said Jinxie. "There's a nice big lake a few levels down where we used to go swimming all the time, but then my cousin Blunkett dropped some cave slugs in it to see what they would do. They stopped glowing once they were in the water. Maybe that's what made them so nasty, because the biggest slug ate the others and got even bigger. It kept eating until it was huge. Blunkett went down to check on him a few weeks later and the thing ate him. We haven't gone down there since."

"And yet trolls are going to the deeper levels," said Aislin. "I need to find out what they're doing."

"We can take you close to the trolls," offered Smax. "You'll get there faster if we show you the way. But I'll tell you now, we won't have anything to do with them. We don't even play tricks on them anymore. Trolls are nasty to begin with, but even nastier when they get riled."

"I understand," Aislin said. She'd had her own bad experiences with trolls. "And I thank you for your offer." Even though she was sure she'd have no problem finding her way anywhere in the mountain, she'd learned from her visits to Deephold that politeness went a long way with spriggans. "That would be very helpful."

One after the other, the spriggans picked up the lanterns they'd set on the ground. None of the lanterns were lit, but as soon as the spriggans shook them, they glowed with a warm yellow light.

"Follow us," said Jinxie, and they set off at a brisk trot. Aislin had to hurry to keep up.

Chapter 2

Aislin was worried. She had sensed fire in the belly of the mountain, but not smoke that could damage the mountain itself. Yet there it was, just a few levels down—smoke where there shouldn't be any, staining rock and damaging it enough to impede its growth. The trolls must have been there with their torches.

As the spriggans led the way down the steep tunnel to the level just below, Aislin sharpened her focus on the chamber where smoke was spreading across the rock face. She could sense other, more violent, things happening, too. A calcite ribbon breaking, the tip of a stalactite snapping off, and fragile rock shattering. Vandals were in the cave, destroying formations that had taken eons to grow.

"Hurry!" Aislin yelled to the spriggans when they reached more level flooring. They all began to run.

Long before they reached the next level, Aislin could smell the smoke and hear harsh, gutteral voices. The intruders were indeed trolls, and it sounded as if there were three of them. As she descended, the smell of the trolls themselves began to reach her, too; the cloying stench was more potent than the smoke. Even from a distance, it was enough to make her stomach roil.

"Stay here, please," Aislin told the spriggans. She pushed past them to follow the smell, tracing the trolls' passage through the tunnels and caves with her mind. The trolls were walking through the maze as if they knew where they were going, through new openings that led them on the safest path while ignoring the more obvious, yet more dangerous, routes. Aislin couldn't understand how they knew where to turn— until she almost tripped over a knotted rope leading from one cave to the next. There were marks on the walls, too, made of chalk or mud and sometimes what looked like old blood. More than one non-pedrasi had explored these caves and left signs for others to follow. Aislin wondered if it had been other trolls. When she examined the walls more closely, she saw fresh smoke stains, as well as some that had been there for years.

Aislin frowned. The pedrasi had claimed these mountains generations ago. Even if they were no longer living in this mountain, it still belonged to them. Spriggans were always welcome, but trolls had no right to be here. Aislin cut the rope with her knife, grimacing at the smell still clinging to the sticky strands. She picked up the end, coiling it as she walked. She would take care of the rest of the rope— as well as the marks on the walls—later. Right now, she had to see where the trolls were going and find out what they had planned.

Soon after reaching a point where the passage slanted downward, Aislin began to hear the trolls well enough to understand what they were saying.

"Don't know why Gringle had to come," one of the trolls grumbled. "Gringle here last time."

"That why!" exclaimed another troll. "Gringle know way. Squint and Ploot never here before."

"Why Gringle not bring dregs back?" asked the third troll.

"Gringle explorer," said Gringle.

"Gringle not bring bags, Ploot," explained Squint. "Need bags for dregs."

What are dregs? Aislin wondered. She stayed far enough behind the trolls that she could still hear them, but they wouldn't be able to see her. Although she wasn't afraid to confront them when it was time, she wasn't going to do it until she'd learned why they were in the mountain.

Aislin followed the arguing trolls as the rope led them farther down. They passed more than one turn-off that looked promising, but Aislin sensed that the tunnels led to deep pits or crevices with sharp rocks at the bottom. Finally reaching the end of the rope, she carried the coil to a deep crevice and tossed it over the edge.

The entrance to the next tunnel heading downward would have been easy to miss. It didn't look like an opening; its walls perfectly matched those of the tunnel she was in. The smoke was thicker here, however, as if the trolls had paused to look around. She could sense the gap before she could see it. When she reached out with her hand, it went right through, so she closed her eyes and let her senses guide her.

The long tunnel led down in a gradual slope.

Soon Aislin could hear the trolls' voices echo, and she knew they'd reached a huge cavern. She sensed that there was a large volume of water there—more than she'd detected anywhere else in the mountain. The fairy light bobbed ahead of her as she walked, but before she got too close, she plucked it from the air and tucked it back in her bag, fearing it might betray her presence.

Moving in complete darkness, Aislin crept to the end of the tunnel and peeked into the cavern. The trolls were on the other side of a lake that filled most of the cavern floor; it looked as if they were heading to a tunnel directly opposite from where Aislin was standing. The light of the trolls' torches reflected off the water, making it look as if another set of them were walking upside down in the lake. Stalactites hung from the ceiling; their wet surfaces glistened as an occasional drip fell into the water with a soft *plunk*. When the water stilled, it was so clear that Aislin could see the rocky bottom. Although she couldn't tell the depth of the lake just by looking, her senses told her that it was more than twenty feet.

Something stirred in the lake, sending ripples that made the reflections shimmer and contort.

Aislin peered deeper into the water. She froze when movement caught her gaze. It was a pale, eel-like creature, over four times as long as she was tall, circling around the lake.

The trolls began to shout at each other, causing Aislin to look up. "Squint go first," cried Gringle. "Gringle not wanna."

"Squint not wanna, too," Squint replied.

"No look at Ploot!" shouted Ploot. "Ploot go last."

One troll shoved another, who stumbled against the cavern wall, knocking off a chunk of calcite ribbon. Both were still shouting when suddenly a patch of the wall lit up. None of the trolls seemed to notice, though, and they soon shambled into the other tunnel, disappearing from sight.

When she was sure that the trolls were gone, Aislin tiptoed around the edge of the lake to the still-glowing patch on the wall. She was surprised to find cave slugs, each as thick around as her thumb, covering the surface. Some were lit up, while others were as dark as the wall itself. Aislin poked a glowing slug with her finger and it glowed even brighter. When she poked a dark one with her finger, it lit up with a flash, settling into a steady yellow glow.

Certain that she had discovered the spriggans' light source, Aislin picked up the calcite that had fallen to the ground. She drew energy from the stone around her and made the calcite thin enough to be translucent while reshaping it into a ball big enough to hold a half dozen of the slugs. After making an opening on one side, she plucked some cave slugs from the wall and dropped them in. When she made the calcite reform over the opening, the ball gave off a warm glow.

Aislin wanted to study the slugs, but now wasn't the time, so she took her fairy light out of her bag and tucked the calcite ball in its place. The fairy light had just begun to bob over her head when she heard a splash. Aislin turned and gasped. The eel-creature was hurling itself at the lake's edge, its circular jaws gaping wide and its three rows of jagged teeth glinting in the glow of her light. The creature seemed to be able to see although it had no eyes.

Water sloshed over the stone floor as Aislin backed toward the next tunnel, her heart racing. Although she was terrified, she couldn't help but wonder what had attracted the beast, which seemed to be tracking the movement of the fairy light. *Even if it can see, it isn't light that attracts it*, she thought. It hadn't reacted to the trolls' torches or the cave slugs' glow.

Reaching the tunnel mouth, Aislin glanced at the fairy light. With a wave of her hand, she sent it floating out over the water. The creature leapt straight up, nearly catching the light in its mouth.

"It must be attracted to magic," Aislin murmured.

She paused to listen as one of the trolls shouted, "Stop shoving!" from inside the tunnel.

Aislin gestured to call the fairy light back to her and let it lead the way as she followed the trolls once again.

Chapter 3

THE FAIRY LIGHT ZIGGED and zagged to avoid protruding rocks as it headed down the descending tunnel. Aislin had used her senses to learn what lay ahead, so she expected to see small pools of warm water steaming in the cool air of a large cavern. Before she reached the end of the tunnel, she could feel heat radiating from whatever lay ahead, but she wasn't expecting the blast of heat that assailed her as she reached the entrance. Small pools pocked the cavern floor, and the water that filled them wasn't just warm—it was boiling. Already perspiring, she knew that she couldn't stay there for long.

Looking around, she saw that the trolls stood

only yards away, clustered around a mound of strange-looking rocks. Reaching out with her mind, Aislin realized that they weren't rocks, but something organic. Noticing the trolls had their backs turned to her, she slipped from the tunnel and silently made her way around the perimeter of the cavern. Approaching another grouping of the objects, she crept close enough to examine one. It was as long as her arm and a dull green color, covered with pale brown bumps.

Aislin gasped. These were dragon eggs, and there were dozens of them rimming the pools of water.

One of the trolls bent down to pick up an egg. After sniffing it, he gave it a good, hard shake. "Dreg hatch soon," the troll announced. Aislin recognized Squint by his voice. "Be extra tasty."

"Yum!" Ploot exclaimed, picking up an egg. "Eat lots!"

"Not lots," said Gringle. "Save for her. Here, put in bag." He handed bags to the other two trolls and stuffed an egg in his own.

Aislin was horrified. Not only were the trolls trespassing, but they were going to steal precious dragon eggs. It sounded as if they intended to eat some of these "dregs" and give the rest to a mysterious "her."

Drawing power from the stone, Aislin summoned her most commanding voice. "Put those down!"

Most kinds of magic didn't work on trolls, so Aislin didn't really expect them to obey, but at least they stopped what they were doing and gaped at her. She stepped forward to confront them and was opening her mouth to speak again when the far wall of the cave seemed to move.

Wiping the sweat from her eyes, Aislin peered at the wall, trying to see what was moving. It blended in with the wall so well that it was almost impossible but, could it be...? And then it moved again and she could suddenly see quite clearly. It was a dragon! Steam puffed from its enormous nostrils as it raised its head and lunged at the trolls. The trolls hadn't noticed the dragon at first, but when they saw the startled expression on Aislin's face, they all turned around.

"Dragon!" Squint bellowed as the dragon's jaws closed around him. There was a loud crunch, cutting off the sound of the troll's rage.

The other trolls screamed and dropped the bags on the ground. They were running toward the tunnel entrance when the dragon roared and blew out the torches, plunging the cavern into darkness. Aislin stood her ground, not sure what to do as the dragon stalked after the trolls, blocking her escape.

Although she couldn't see the dragon, she could hear its talons scrape the rock floor and its scales rasp against the walls. The trolls were still screaming as they ran up the tunnel. Luckily for them, it was too narrow for the dragon to enter. Taking a deep breath, the giant lizard shoved its head into the hole and roared again. The trolls' screaming grew louder for a moment, then faded as they kept running.

The dragon turned to face Aislin. When it hissed and lunged in her direction, she darted to the side, easily avoiding the rocks. As she hurried around the next bubbling pool, Aislin could hear its jaws snap shut right where she had been standing.

"Hold still, egg thief," the dragon said in a husky, but decidedly female, voice. "You can't escape me. I'll make your death quick if you stop running."

"I'm not an egg thief!" Aislin protested, hurrying out of the way when the dragon's head whipped toward her. She sidestepped a stalagmite to narrowly avoid the beast's next lunge. Sensing that a grouping of the formations lay ahead, she crept behind them, then drew power from the rock to join the stalagmites on the floor of the cave with the stalactites hanging overhead. The columns that took shape in front of her were still thickening when the dragon took a deep breath and exhaled flame in her general direction. Aislin drew back, but the columns blocked the flame from reaching her.

"I am not an egg thief," Aislin repeated from behind her wall of rock. "I am pedrasi and would never hurt your eggs."

The dragon hissed. Its talons clicked against the stone as it came closer. "Pedrasi have not visited this mountain for many years. How do I know that you speak the truth?"

Aislin wondered if the dragon had missed seeing her create the columns. Perhaps it had been too dark and a clearer demonstration would help. Taking out the fairy light, she let it loose. Peering around the column, she made yet another form directly in front of the dragon. The giant lizard whuffed, its eyes growing wide in wonder.

"Who but pedrasi can make rock grow?" Aislin asked. "I was not here to help the trolls; I followed them to see why they had trespassed in a mountain that the pedrasi have long claimed."

"Are you saying that only pedrasi are welcomed here?" asked the dragon, its voice edged with anger.

"Not at all," Aislin protested as she stepped out from behind the column. "Pedrasi do not profess to own the mountains; we are their guardians. As such, we protect them from those who would do them harm. We understand that others have long sheltered in our mountains, and they have every right to do so. Dragons are welcome here, but thieving trolls are not. Trolls are vandals who destroy what they touch."

The dragon sat back on her haunches and nodded. "I have heard about pedrasi, although I have never met any until today. I am young for my kind, and this is my first clutch of eggs."

"All these eggs are yours?" Aislin asked, astonished at their number as she looked around.

The dragon snorted. "No, of course not! Only three are mine. It is my turn to watch over all the eggs my flock laid this year. Soon another dragon will come to take my place and I will leave to hunt. Perhaps I will hunt trolls this time."

"That sounds like a good idea," said Aislin. "And I really should follow the two trolls that just ran out of here to make sure they leave and don't come back."

"How can you prevent them from returning?" asked the dragon. "Do you intend to kill them?"

Aislin shuddered and shook her head. "I have my ways, but killing is not one of them. After they leave, I'll close off the entrance that the trolls used. It will take them a long time to find another way in. I know there are many, including the one that I sense is big enough for dragons. I will make sure that that entrance stays open. It should be safer for you and your eggs now. When he hears trolls have been coming here, I'm sure my grandfather will want to set up patrols to keep them away."

"Thank you, pedrasi girl," said the dragon. "I am Singea of the blue dragon line. What is your name so that I may tell my kin about what you have done?"

"I am Aislin of the pedrasi and fairy lines," she replied. "And you are very welcome. Before I go, I need to heal the smoke damage on the walls. The trolls were careless with their torches and I need to fix what I can."

The dragon looked contrite when she said, "I am sorry if I added to the damage. I was just so angry when I saw those monsters touching the eggs."

"I understand," Aislin told her. "It would be enough to make any mother angry."

Chapter 4

THE TUNNEL LEADING BACK to the lake was fairly straight, with only a few bends near the end. The trolls had made it all the way through even without a torch to light their path, but Aislin doubted they could have made it to the other side of the lake in the absolute dark. She reached the end of the tunnel sooner than she'd expected. When she looked for the trolls, they were only a third of the way around the lake, feeling their way by running their hands along the cavern wall and grumbling as they went.

"Squint dumb. Not run like us," said Ploot. His voice rang out in the silence of the cavern.

"What that?" Gringle asked, pointing at the fairy light floating in front of Aislin.

The trolls stared at Aislin and her light. In a second, they were running toward her, slipping and sliding on the wet floor. "Girl got light! Ploot want!" cried Ploot.

"Eat girl!" cried Gringle.

"Get girl and light!" shouted Ploot.

Suddenly Kimble appeared from behind an outcropping, as if erupting out of the stone itself. Startled, Aislin froze, but Kimble darted forward to pluck the fairy light from the air. "You want the light, you can have it!" the spriggan girl shouted to the trolls, tossing the light at the troll closest to the water's edge. "Here, catch!"

Ploot snatched the light from the air and held it out so his friend couldn't grab it from him. When the troll glanced at Aislin and the spriggan, his ugly face twisted into something hideous. "Now eat you both!" he growled.

The trolls had taken only a few more steps when the eel-creature suddenly leapt out of the water and clamped its jaws around Ploot. The cave went dark as the troll and the fairy light disappeared down the beast's gullet, though Aislin could see a faint glow descend into its belly. With an enormous splash, the creature dove to the bottom of the lake. The remaining troll bellowed in fear and stumbled against the walls, wailing as he fought to find his way out of the cavern.

"Do fairy lights ever go out?" Kimble asked Aislin as they peered into the water, watching the glow inside the beast move from one side of the lake to the other.

Aislin shook her head. "It would if I told it to, but other than that, I don't think so."

"Good!" said Kimble. "Then we'll always be able to locate Old Grumpy, and he won't be able to sneak up on us again. What happened to the other troll?"

"A dragon ate it," Aislin told her.

"I didn't think you'd killed it," Kimble replied. "Pedrasi aren't known for being vicious."

Aislin opened the sack she was carrying, took out the calcite light, and shook it. The cave slugs squirmed inside and the ball lit, giving off a soft yellow glow. When Aislin looked again, the troll had disappeared up the other tunnel. Glancing at the creature in the lake one last time, she said, "I'm glad the fairy light will be useful down there, because I wasn't about to go after it."

She turned to look at Kimble. "I thought spriggans never came to this level."

"We don't, unless a pedrasi princess is in danger," Kimble replied.

"Thank you, although I could have handled it myself," said Aislin.

Kimble laughed. "I'm sure you're right, but my way took care of the troll for good. Spriggans don't have anything against trolls unless they come inside our mountain. Now that troll will never bother anyone again."

"I need to see what happened to the other troll," Aislin told her.

"My friends are up there. They'll take care of it," said Kimble.

Aislin frowned and said, "That's what worries me."

When Aislin and Kimble reached the top of the tunnel, Gringle was nowhere in sight, but the spriggans were waiting with their lamps lit. They looked nervous as they peered down into the tunnel behind Aislin. "Only one troll came up," Jinxie told her. "Where are the others?"

"They won't be coming up," said Kimble. "They met with unfortunate accidents. When the troll came out of the tunnel, where did he go?"

"Into the maze," Jinxie said. When a horrible wailing sound came from that direction, he added, "He's probably lost already."

"He'll wander around in there forever!" Borry announced, sounding gleeful. "My old pappy told tales of the people who came poking around in the mountain and got good and lost. You can still see their bones in that maze."

"I can't believe my ancestors would allow that to happen!" Aislin exclaimed, horrified.

Smax shrugged. "The pedrasi were gone by then, so they weren't here to stop it."

"Well, I am," said Aislin. "I don't intend to let that poor creature 'wander around in there forever.'" Closing her eyes, she searched for the quickest way out for the troll.

"What is she doing?" Jinxie whispered.

"Maybe she's in a trance. Do you think she can hear us?" asked Smax.

"I can hear you just fine," Aislin told them with her eyes still closed. "Please be quiet and don't move. I have to concentrate and I don't want to crush you by accident."

Aislin's hair began to crackle as she drew more and more power from the rock. She had moved rock this way before, but not on such a large scale. Unsure that she could even do what she had planned, she knew that she'd need a lot more power if she was even going to attempt it. If it worked, it would be the quickest way she could think of to get the troll out of the mountain unharmed. A frightened troll would be more valuable than an injured one; an injured troll would be back with friends seeking revenge, while a frightened troll might be enough to keep others away from the mountain.

The spriggans shuffled their feet, waiting uneasily while Aislin drew more and more power into herself. She could see the glow around her through her closed eyelids as she absorbed more power than she ever had before. Her skin tingled and her heart pounded in her chest, but she didn't stop until her body began to shake with the effort to hold the power in. Then, squeezing her hands into fists, she willed the rock to move, shutting off some openings and revealing others. The mountain groaned and shrieked as rock scraped rock, rearranging passageways that had been there for eons. Moving the rock around Gringle, Aislin herded him through the maze to the cave entrance that she herself had used. Frightened, the troll wailed as it ran.

Perspiration beaded Aislin's forehead when the troll finally stumbled out of the mountain and staggered down the slope. With the last remains of the power she'd pulled into herself, she sealed off the entrance as if it had never existed. Although she was exhausted, she couldn't help but smile. She had surprised herself by doing something that she hadn't even known for sure that she could do. Apparently, taking the time to gather power first made a big difference.

"Wow!" Kimble said as Aislin opened her eyes and sat down, exhausted. "I don't know what you just did, but it sure sounded like something big. Are you all right?"

Aislin nodded. "I will be. I just need to rest for a while."

"Is the troll gone?" asked Smax.

"He is," said Aislin. "I'm afraid you'll have to relearn your maze. It's not at all like it used to be."

"What is going on here?" a new spriggan asked, stepping out of a large crack in the wall. Aislin hadn't seen him before, though she'd assumed there were more living in the mountain. Suddenly the space around her was filled with spriggans, young and old, some gray with stone dust and others clean and tidy.

"You should have been here, Poppa," said Kimble. "Aislin just rearranged parts of the mountain and got a troll to leave."

"How did she do that?" asked a spriggan with a long beard as straggly as his hair. Although he was the oldest one there, with wrinkled skin and a cane to help him walk, his eyes were bright and he was as covered with stone dust as most of them.

"Aislin is a pedrasi princess!" Jinxie replied. "She can do anything."

Aislin shook her head. "I wouldn't say that. There are a lot of things I can't do." She couldn't help but think of all the fairy abilities she wished she had. "But I did get rid of the troll."

The bearded spriggan frowned. "My name is Winholt and I'm the Elder of Mount Gora. Whatever you did to the mountain, it's probably unstable now and we'll all have to leave."

Aislin shook her head. "It's not unstable. I was very careful. I even shored up some of the weaker parts near a waterfall."

"I'll go look," another spriggan said, and ran off, holding a lantern in front of him.

Winholt wasn't entirely convinced. "You're a pedrasi princess? You don't look like a pedrasi."

Aislin sighed. "I get that a lot. Like I told the others, my grandfather is King Talus. I'm half pedrasi and half fairy."

"If your grandfather is the king, you should be able to read pedrasi," Winholt told her. "What does that say?" He pointed to something carved into the wall above the entrance to another tunnel.

Aislin studied it for a moment. The words were hard to read because so many of them were spelled oddly, but she finally read out loud, "This way to the baths. Be considerate of others. They want clean water, too."

A spriggan snorted and clapped another on the back. "That means you, Spillip! You always leave a mess behind."

Aislin chuckled, but knew she had to get on her way. "I'm sorry, but I have a lot of work to do and I'd like to get started," she told them. "I want to remove the smoke stains from the trolls' torches and clean up the rubble they left behind."

"If you're here, are the pedrasi coming back to live in the mountain?" asked a spriggan from the back of the group.

"Not as far as I know," Aislin replied. "But I'm going to suggest that my grandfather start sending patrols to make sure that everything is all right. If anything comes up and you want to contact him, you can send him messages through the patrols."

The spriggan holding the lantern came running back. "She was right! The weak places near the waterfall are a lot stronger now." Aislin could tell the group was impressed.

"We can help you clean up," Kimble told Aislin. "What do you need us to do?"

"You could pick up the rubble," Aislin replied.

"What about the smoke stains?" asked Smax.

Aislin glanced at the stains on the ceiling. "Leave those to me. I have an idea that might work."

She had been thinking about it ever since she saw the first stain. Although she was bone-achingly tired, she didn't want to take the time to rest, so she drew power into herself once more and sent it back into the smoke-damaged rocks. Her first effort sheared off a chunk of rock, but with each attempt she took less and less, fine-tuning her skill until she was able to remove only the smoke-stained layers, leaving clean, healthy rock behind. Kimble put herself in charge of the dust-cleanup crew and made sure that the spriggans were thorough.

Aislin followed the route that the trolls had taken,

removing the damaged rock while the spriggans swept up behind her. She worked as far as the tunnel leading to the lake, but didn't go near the cavern. It didn't take her long to finish.

Returning to the level where she'd entered the mountain, she closed her eyes once more and finished creating a map of Mount Gora in her mind. She also located three other exits that she could use. When she was finished, she turned to the spriggans who had been following her and said, "Thank you for your help, and please give my thanks to the others who helped as well."

"Do you think you'll ever come back?" asked Kimble.

Aislin smiled at her. "I will, as soon as I can. And maybe someday you can come visit me in Deephold."

"I'd love that!" Kimble cried, grinning from ear to ear. "I want to see every part of Deephold. Do you think the pedrasi will like me?"

"I think they'll like you a lot," Aislin told her. "Especially after I tell them how much you helped me."

Chapter 5

THAT MORNING IT HAD taken Aislin nearly an hour to go from the spot where she'd left Twinket and the pedrasi guards to the opening into the mountain. Leaving the mountain was a different story, however. The new exit was more than two hours from their campsite and forced her to skirt tall boulders and pick her way over rough terrain to reach them.

It was early evening by the time Aislin finally saw the campsite. She was surprised to find that the only ones there were Twinket and two of the six guards. The collars of their stone-gray tunics bore the war hammer emblem of the pedrasi royals. One of the guards was a pedrasi girl named Tourmaline who everyone called Lin. She was shorter than Aislin and was muscular from all her intensive training. Like all pedrasi warriors, she wore her black hair cut short so it would fit in her helmet. Although Lin was only four years older than the princess, she was a full-fledged warrior.

The other guard was an orc girl, Deela. Taller and broader of shoulder than either a pedrasi or a fairy, she had tusks that curled up alongside her jaw and a pronounced ridge of bone above her eyebrows. Her hair was coarser, too, and was brown mixed with black. Like all orcs, Deela had been trained to fight as soon as she could walk. She was only three years older than Aislin and was already considered one of the fiercest warriors of Deephold. Lin had been born at Deephold, but Deela had been ten when she'd arrived at the mountain stronghold. Aislin had known both of them for much of her life.

Twinket looked up hearing Aislin's approach, while the two guards raised their weapons. When they saw that it was the princess, Twinket jumped to her feet and the guards hurried to greet her.

Aislin nodded to Lin and Deela. Glancing at the campsite, she frowned and asked, "Where are the others?"

Twinket was still clutching the necklace that Aislin had left with her that morning. "We heard all that racket in the mountain, and then the opening you'd used closed up and they got all worried. I looked at your necklace and told them you were fine," the doll explained, "and Lin and Deela believed me, but the others wouldn't listen and went running off all worked up and worried." The stone pendant, a gift from Aislin's fairy grandmother, was in tune with the princess's moods, changing color as her mood changed. Anyone who saw the necklace could tell exactly what Aislin was feeling.

"The others left right away, but we waited when Twinket showed us the stone. We were concerned when it went red for a moment. When the color changed, we knew you could handle whatever you were facing," added Deela.

"Those pedrasi men are new to Deephold and don't know you like we do," said Lin. "You are all right, aren't you?"

"I'm fine," Aislin said, taking a seat by the fire. "Just hungry and tired." She covered her mouth, yawning. "I did what I needed to do. I'll give my grandfather a full report when I see him."

Aislin closed her eyes for a moment. When she

opened them, Lin was offering her a plate piled with hot food and a cup of warm cider. Twinket stood by her feet, looking worried. "You went to sleep awfully fast. Are you all right? You didn't get hit on the head or anything and get a concession?"

"You mean concussion, and no, I didn't," Aislin replied, and yawned again. "Like I said, I'm just really tired." Her hands shook with fatigue as she took a sip of cider. She had only swallowed a bite of panfried fish and one of bread when her eyes drifted shut again.

Aislin woke the next morning to Twinket prying her eyelid open and staring into her eye from only inches away. "What are you doing?" Aislin asked, jerking her head to the edge of the pallet.

"I was checking to see if you were alive," said Twinket. "The stone on your necklace was an odd color and you were making funny sounds. You stopped all of a sudden and I was worried."

"Don't ever do that again!" Aislin said, rubbing her eyelids with her knuckles.

"Ok," the little doll said, hopping off the bed. "I'll think of something else next time."

"Ahem," Deela said outside her tent flap. "If you're awake, Your Highness, we have breakfast ready. The other guards are back and ready to go. We can travel farther if we get an early start."

"I'll be right there," Aislin replied. "I'd like to reach Deephold as soon as we can. I have a lot to tell the king."

"So do I," said Twinket. "Like how he needs to send better pillows the next time we have to sleep in a tent. The one you were using was lumpy. I hardly got any sleep on it."

After a quick breakfast, the small group headed down the mountain. It was early enough that dew glistened on the wildflowers and the songbirds were still greeting the new day. At first the plants were scrubby and low to the ground, but after a while the party entered a copse of slender trees. It wasn't long before they were in a pine forest and had to wend their way between the trees single file, with Aislin in the middle of the group and Twinket riding on her shoulder. Aislin was thinking about the map of Mount Gora and how she would draw it for her grandfather, when suddenly something big and brown picked her up and squeezed the breath out of her.

"Ugh!" she yelped.

"Hey, watch it!" Twinket cried as the creature knocked her to the ground.

"Unhand the princess!" shouted Lin.

The brown creature gave Aislin one last squeeze before setting her down. Aislin took a deep, shuddering breath and looked up at her assailant. She knew right away that it was a Big Foot, because they often visited her parents' castle. "Fluffy?" she said. It was hard to distinguish one from another because they were all covered in brown fur. Fluffy had fluffier fur than most, however, so it was quite possible that this was Aislin's friend.

"'Tis I." The Big Foot nodded and patted Aislin's head. Although Aislin knew that Fluffy was very sweet, the Big Foot was over seven feet tall and had hands and feet as big as frying pans, making her look intimidating.

"Put your hands in the air and back away from the princess," said Deela.

Fluffy grunted and put up her hands. She winked at Aislin as she backed away.

"It's all right," Aislin said when she noticed that the guards had their weapons out. "I know Fluffy. She didn't mean any harm."

"What about me?" Twinket asked, brushing off her gown. "I'm not all right! I landed on some pokey pine needles and now my gown is sticky with pine sap."

"Sorry about that," said Fluffy.

"No one is supposed to touch a member of the royal family without express permission," said Lin.

"Fluffy has my permission," Aislin told her, then lowered her voice to say to the Big Foot, "though please try not to hug me so hard next time. What are you doing here?"

"I was about to ask you that very thing," said Fluffy. "I was on my morning stroll when who should I see but my old friend, Princess Aislin, who I hear is now the hero of the kingdom. A little bird told me that you let humans kidnap you to protect your family and everyone in the castle. Is that true, or was that finch making up stories again?"

"It's true," Aislin confessed. "But I'm back now and everything is fine."

"I can see that," Fluffy said with a grin. "Are the

fairies returning to the human kingdoms or is that just a nasty rumor?"

"They're going back," Aislin told her. "And it's going to happen soon."

"But your parents are staying in their castle, right? I really like your home and visiting it is such fun! I don't like humans, though. Most of them don't think Big Foots are real. My great grandfather says that he moved to the land between the mountains because the humans that saw him tried to shoot him with arrows. You couldn't pay me enough to move back there."

"My parents are staying right where they are," Aislin reassured her.

"Good!" Fluffy declared. "Then you can count on me to visit again soon. I've been thinking about taking a nice long walk."

Fluffy waved goodbye as they continued on. Twinket watched her from atop Aislin's shoulder and seemed relieved when the Big Foot was out of sight. "I don't like Fluffy," Twinket told Aislin. "Her fur tickles my nose and makes me sneeze. Plus, she smells funny."

"She smells like pine trees," said Aislin.

"That's what I mean," Twinket told her. "Only

fairies should smell like plants. Uh oh, look straight ahead. There's a bunch of gnomes waiting by the edge of the path. What do you suppose *they* want?"

The pine forest was merging with a stand of oak trees, which meant that they were entering the valley that led to Sweet River. A stream meandered along one side of the path while the other side was thick with knee-high ferns. The ferns looked as if they were blossoming with dots of red and yellow, purple and blue. Both Aislin and Poppy knew that the bright colors weren't really flowers; they were gnomes' pointed caps.

"Greetings!" called a gnome, stepping onto the path. His bright red cap stood out like a beacon and would have been hard to miss.

The guards stopped walking to gather around the princess as if to protect her. "You don't need to guard me from gnomes!" Aislin cried. "Let him approach."

"Maybe I should do the talking," Twinket whispered into her ear. "I don't think we know him."

"Then it's time I met him," said Aislin. "I don't need your help, Twinket."

"We'll see about that," the little doll muttered.

"Welcome to Joyful Valley, Your Highness," the gnome said as he drew close. Like all older male gnomes, he had white hair, a long, white beard, and a flowing white mustache. He also had twinkling blue eyes and a grin that made Aislin want to smile, too. Even his voice seemed to have a smile in it. "We heard you were coming this way, so my family and friends have come to witness this historic moment."

"Thank you," said Aislin. "I'm delighted to meet all of you."

"Word has spread about how valiantly you strove to defend your castle by letting the humans take you away. We have relatives who live in the castle, so we owe you our personal thanks. My name is Bobble. You may know my brother, Gambol."

"Of course, I know Gambol," Aislin replied. She knew everyone in her parents' castle. Gambol was in charge of the stables and had a real way with animals. "I'm delighted to meet you, Bobble."

The gnome bowed and backed away while gesturing toward the ferns. "And these are my family and friends," he said, prompting a flood of gnomes to step onto the path.

Though most of the adults bowed and waved at

Aislin, the gnome children jumped up and down to get her attention. Aislin was surprised when a gnome mother held up her baby and said, "Please kiss her for luck!"

Aislin smiled and bent down to kiss the baby. When the tiny infant cooed and gurgled, all the gnomes laughed and applauded. After that, the rest of the mothers held up their babies, expecting them to be kissed as well. It wasn't until Aislin had kissed all the infants and patted all the children on their heads and shaken the hand of every adult that the gnomes finally moved out of her way so she could continue on.

"I counted one hundred thirty-two gnomes," Twinket told Aislin as they walked through the valley. "Although I may have missed a few. Just how big is a gnome's family?"

"It varies," said Aislin. "They weren't all his family. Some of them were his friends."

Twinket laughed. "That's still a lot of gnomes in one place!"

Soon the pine trees gave way to maples and oaks. Decaying leaves cushioned the party's steps and the sun's rays filtered down to light their way. Aislin was enjoying the scent of loam and growing things when a cloud of tiny fairies descended on the group. The guards stopped once again to cluster around Aislin, eyeing the fairies closet to them.

"Oh, for flowers' sake!" Twinket cried. "Now what?"

Unlike the gnomes, the fairies didn't look happy. As they all changed from tiny to human-sized, a fairy dressed in blue petals scowled. "We heard you were coming this way, and we wanted to talk to you. We're not at all happy that King Darinar and Queen Surinen have declared that we're moving back to live among the humans. We like it here! We don't want to move, but nobody asked what we want."

"You royals think you can play with our lives as if we don't matter," said a fairy in a cap made of daisies. "We were perfectly content in our old home when your grandparents made us move here. And now just hundreds of years later you want us to move back again. We might as well not unpack if you're going to make us move around so much!"

Aislin was surprised. She hadn't known that any-one felt this way. Of course, some fey would want to stay, but no one had said that they couldn't! Long ago, the king and queen of the fairies had ordered all the fey to go with them to the land between the mountains. Now that they were returning to their ancestral home in the human lands, they were letting the fey decide if they wanted to stay or go.

"That's right!" declared a fairy with fuzzy green hair. "We've heard that it's all your fault. If you hadn't gone to the human land to check it out, we wouldn't be moving back there!"

Shocked, Aislin's eyes grew wide. True, she had gone to the human lands, but only to protect her family from curious humans. While there, she had investigated what was going on. Though the things she had learned had influenced her grandparents' decision to return, Aislin was sure that it hadn't been based on what she did or didn't like.

"Don't answer them," Twinket told the princess. "They shouldn't talk to you that way."

"They can talk to me if they want to," Aislin told the doll before turning back to the fairies. "Don't you see—you have a choice now. You can stay here or go back. Whether or not you move is up to you."

"We need to go," said Twinket. "We'll never get to Deephold at this rate."

"I'm sorry this whole thing upset you," Aislin

called to the fairies as her guards pushed them to the side and ushered her down the path.

"You can never make everyone happy," Twinket declared.

"You don't need to be rude to them, though," Aislin told her.

"Hey, I'm only trying to protect you!" said Twinket. "I think I should be rude more often."

"Please don't," Aislin replied. Dealing with fey complaints was hard enough without Twinket butting in and being less than civil.

The guards refused to let anyone else approach the princess as they made their way through the valley. It didn't stop them from trying, though. More fairies came by, demanding to know why they had to move; a satyr called Aislin unkind names, and a sprite dropped down from the treetops to berate the princess. Each time, the guards chased them off and hurried the princess away.

Eventually they reached the spot where two other streams joined the first, forming Sweet River. Aislin and her guards had just turned south to walk beside the river when a blue-haired nymph popped up in the swiftly moving water. "Hi, Princess!" she called. "How you doing? I heard that you showed real courage around those nasty humans. Great job! We're all really proud of you."

"At least this one is being nice," said Twinket.

The nymph frowned. "Has someone been unkind to you, Your Highness?"

"It seems that some fey aren't happy that my grandparents plan to move the castle back to the human lands," Aislin said as the nymph kept pace with them.

"And they have the nerve to blame Aislin!" cried Twinket.

"Well, I never!" the nymph exclaimed. "The king and queen have every right to move if they want to, like anyone else. I change rivers every few years just to keep life interesting. And I don't understand why they'd blame you. All you did was save your family and all the fey in the castle. Then you found out what was really going on with the humans, which someone needed to do. You didn't do anything wrong, and anyone who says differently is a two-headed frog."

"Uh, thank you ..." said Aislin.

"That was very well said," Twinket told the nymph. "If only the knuckleheads who keep wanting to complain to Aislin would leave us alone."

"Maybe I can help with that," the nymph told her and disappeared into the water.

Aislin wondered what the nymph could possibly do, but forgot about her offer when she didn't reappear right away. As they walked along the river, the princess couldn't help but wonder how many fey blamed her for their unhappiness. Suddenly, a loud splash drew her gaze to the water where she spotted a group of heads bobbing close to shore. The nymph was back, along with her friends, and each one was dragging a bundle of reeds or some sturdy pieces of driftwood. Dumping their finds on the riverbank, the nymphs quickly assembled a raft big enough to carry Aislin and her guards down the river.

"Now you can ride the river all the way to Deephold," said the blue-haired nymph.

"That's so kind of you," Aislin told her as the guards piled on.

"It's the least we can do for the hero of the land between the mountains!" another nymph declared.

Aislin took a seat on the raft while the guards used long poles to keep them floating in the middle of the river and away from the shoreline. Some of the nymphs followed to the first bend in the river, where they waved goodbye before disappearing underwater.

"This is fun!" Twinket announced from her seat on Aislin's lap. "The last time you went on a boat, I had to stay in a satchel. Have I ever told you how much I hate traveling that way? Tiny spaces scare me. I really like traveling this way, though. It's a lot faster than walking, and we can see so much! How long will it take us to reach Deephold now?"

"We're moving at a good clip," said Deela. "We should be there before nightfall if we keep this up."

"That's too bad," said Twinket. "I could float like this forever."

Aislin enjoyed floating down the river, too. Not only was it fun to see everything from the water, but it meant that they could drift past the fey who had gathered along the riverbank. By the time the party finally approached Deephold, Aislin was more than ready to avoid any more confrontations.

As the guards landed the raft at the base of the mountain, Aislin climbed off with Twinket in her arms. She didn't notice the pink-haired fairy waiting just outside the main entrance into the mountain until the fairy called out to her.

"You're breaking up my family!" the fairy shouted as the guards tried to keep them separated. "My parents want to go back to their old home, but my husband wants to stay here. I don't know what to do. If you hadn't gone to the human world and gotten all nosy, your grandparents wouldn't have even thought about going back. This whole thing is your fault!"

Aislin sighed. Here was someone else who blamed her, when all she'd been trying to do was help. Didn't they know enough about her grandparents to realize that they were doing what they thought best for all the fey? And why in the name of all that blossomed couldn't they leave her alone?

"Can't you stay here with your husband and visit your parents once in a while?" Aislin asked the fairy. "It's not as if King Darinar and Queen Surinen are moving their palace to the other side of the world."

"I suppose," said the fairy. "That would be like a vacation, and we've never taken a vacation before."

The fairy looked more thoughtful than angry when Aislin turned away.

The pedrasi were happy to see the princess return, even though she hadn't been gone for long. A footman escorted her through the tunnels to the throne room deep inside the mountain where her grandfather was still holding audience with the last petitioners of the day.

Aislin was glad to be home. She actually had three homes—Deephold; Eliasind, where she lived with her parents and little brother; and Fairengar, the palace where her fairy grandparents lived—and she was just as comfortable in all of them. To ensure that no one felt cheated of her time, her parents had made sure that Aislin had spent equal amounts of her childhood with her pedrasi grandparents and her fairy grandparents. Adept with languages after learning so many from the visitors to the three royal homes, Aislin was comfortable talking to just about anyone and knew a great deal about all the fey.

The gathering hall was only a short distance from the king's throne room. As Aislin passed through the hall, she saw an orc mother bouncing her toddler on her knee. The princess returned the mother's wave hello and smiled when she saw a minotaur calf talking to a pedrasi boy. There were more orcs and minotaurs here than in either of the other royal residences; both species preferred dark corridors over light and airy spaces.

"I need a clean dress," Twinket announced as they left the hall. "This one smells like campfire smoke."

The footman called to a passing maid and told her of the doll's request. "I'll take care of that," the maid replied. "Come with me."

Aislin handed the doll to the maid and tried not to smile when Twinket began demanding everything else she wanted. The princess felt sorry for the maid who was about to become very busy.

As Aislin reached the door to the throne room, the footman who opened it bowed and backed away. When the few remaining petitioners saw her, they excused themselves and left the room. King Talus looked worried as she approached the throne. "You're back so soon!" he cried and got to his feet. "Is something wrong?"

Aislin shook her head. "It didn't take me long to make the map. I had some interesting encounters in the mountain, but that ended well and then we had a little help from some water nymphs on our way back. They made a raft so we could float down the Sweet River. The raft saved us a lot of time and helped us avoid the fey—who, by the way, aren't happy that King Darinar and Queen Surinen are moving their palace back to the human lands. For some reason, the fey seem to blame me."

"How odd," the king said as he descended the steps and took a seat beside her at the bottom. "Why would they blame you for anything? You've done nothing but help the fey."

"I have no idea," said Aislin. "All I want to do is keep everyone safe and help make the move as smooth and easy as possible and now people are accusing me of ruining their lives! I don't understand what I did to get so many fey to turn against me."

"I doubt very much that you did anything wrong," her grandfather said. "Some people are going to be unhappy about the move no matter what, and they want someone to blame. You were able to study Mount Gora. Has it changed much since the last map was made?"

"Yes, in a number of ways. I have a lot to tell you; some things you'll like and some you won't."

"Why don't you start from the beginning?" suggested the king.

And so Aislin did. She told him about the crystal cave and how she had drawn power into herself. She described writing the names with crystal flowers, which he found amusing. When she mentioned hearing knocking, he nodded and said, "Spriggans. I didn't think that anyone lived in Mount Gora. Did you talk to them?"

"I did," said Aislin. "Until I sensed a disturbance in another part of the mountain. That's when they told me that trolls had been visiting the mountain, but they didn't know why. So I went to look."

Her grandfather frowned. "You should never go near trolls."

Aislin tried not to smile. The first time she'd run into trolls, she'd been frightened and had run away with her friends. The second time she'd been alone, and the third time Kimble had joined her; both of those times, the trolls had been the ones to flee.

"I kept my distance," Aislin told her grandfather. "There were three of them and they were heading to a lower level. There's a lake in Mount Gora; an enormous, blind creature lives in it. The spriggans call him Old Grumpy. They've been staying away from the lake ever since the beast ate a spriggan."

Her grandfather's eyebrow shot up. "And the trolls went to the lake?"

Aislin nodded. "They were collecting dragon eggs, which they call dregs. A female dragon was there, and she ate one of the trolls. Her name was Singea. She seemed nice enough once she stopped trying to fry me."

Her grandfather looked worried when he said, "I never would have sent you there if I'd known there were trolls and dragons. I'm so sorry you had to deal with all this."

"I told the spriggans that I was going to ask you to start sending patrols to Mount Gora. I think we need to keep a better eye on it in the future."

"That's a very good idea," said the king. "I'll tell the captain of the guard to start sending a regular patrol. Do you know if the trolls took any dragon eggs? Angry dragons won't be easy to deal with."

"Not even one. And they didn't want the eggs just to eat. They said that 'she' wanted some, so they couldn't eat them all."

"Interesting. I wonder who 'she' is. Go on."

"Two trolls got away. I followed them back to the lake where a spriggan girl named Kimble showed up. After she tossed my fairy light to a troll, Old Grumpy jumped out of the water and ate the troll, light and all.

It seems that the beast is attracted to magic. Old Grumpy is swimming around in the lake with the light glowing inside it now. Oh, and I found these in that cavern." Aislin took out the calcite globe and handed it to the king. It wasn't glowing, so she said, "Shake it."

The king shook the globe and chuckled when it lit up. "Cave slugs! These little things, when put in water, can grow to be quite dangerous. I believe they were the reason that my grandfather moved the pedrasi out of Mount Gora. Cave slugs are generally rare, but Mount Gora seemed to have more than most mountains." He handed the ball of calcite back to her. "Did you make this?"

"I did. I also discovered a way to clean smoke damage off rock walls. The spriggans cleaned up the rubble that the trolls had left behind. Kimble was a big help. Don't be surprised if she shows up here one day. She told me she'd like to visit Deephold."

"She's welcome any time," said the king. "Now, what about the map? Are you prepared to draw it?"

"Yes," said Aislin. "I think I can give you some decent details, too."

"Then follow me," the king said, getting to his

feet. "I have a gift from King Darinar that I'd like you to try."

He led the way through another door into his private study. Taking a box off a shelf, he set it on the table that dominated the room. The box was intricately carved with a map of the mountain range that included both Deephold and Mount Gora. Setting his hands on either side of the box, he pressed two fingers and the lid lifted on its own. A shining silver ball floated out of the box and hovered in front of the king.

"Come stand here," he told Aislin as he stepped out of the way. While she moved to take his place, the king carried the empty box to the far end of the table.

"Now take the ball between your hands and think about the mountain," said the king. "Think about the outside first, then level by level."

Aislin nodded and took a deep breath. The map in her mind was as clear as if she could see it already drawn in front of her. As she thought about the mountain, a three-dimensional model a few feet tall appeared to float above the table. Depth and color filled in the image as the princess thought about the levels. When she was finished, it was so detailed that she could even see the writing on the wall above the tunnel entrance.

"Excellent!" the king announced as Aislin let go of the ball and stepped back from the table. He walked around the image, admiring it from all sides.

"That's the lake where the creature lives," Aislin said, pointing. "And that's where the dragons placed their eggs. This maze isn't at all what it used to be. I rearranged the walls when I chased the last troll out of the mountain."

"You did?" said the king. "I'm very impressed. It sounds as if your abilities are greater than I'd even imagined. You also have a remarkable memory for details."

There was a knock on the door. "You may enter," said the king.

The door opened and a fairy wearing the leaf emblem of the queen's service on his tunic stepped into the room. Ailsin knew him well. Periwinkle, or Peri as everyone called him, was the head messenger for the fairy king and queen. "Your Majesty, Your Highness, Their Majesties King Darinar and Queen Surinen request the presence of Princess Aislin at Fairengar," he said. "I've been instructed that the princess needs to go as soon as possible."

King Talus nodded. "I was expecting this, although not quite so soon. King Darinar told me that they'll be moving back to the human part of the world in a few days. All right, my love. Go see Queen Amethyst first. Your grandmother would never forgive either of us if you didn't say goodbye. Then get ready to go to Fairengar. You're about to see history in the making."

Chapter 6

"BUT I HAVE TO go, too!" Twinket cried as Peri led the way to a balcony overlooking the valley far below.

"I have just enough fairy dust for one," the fairy told her. "The dust the queen gave me to use for the princess is hard to find. I don't have enough for two separate sprinkles."

"But if I'm holding Twinket, won't she shrink with me?" asked Aislin.

The fairy scowled, as if deep in thought. "I guess so," he finally said. "But if it doesn't work and I can't shrink you, you'll have to ride a mountain pony instead of a dragonfly. It will be your fault if you're late."

"I'll take all the blame if I don't get there as quickly as Queen Surinen wants, but I don't think you need to worry," said Aislin. She adjusted the doll in her arms, then looked up at Peri. "I'm ready."

Peri sighed and shook his head even as he opened the pouch. Dumping the contents into his hand, he sprinkled it over Aislin and stepped back. Pale purple dust sparkled around her for a moment, then suddenly she was tiny.

Although she was half pedrasi and half fairy, Aislin took mostly after her pedrasi side and shared their abilities, which her fairy side only seemed to enhance. For much of her life, Aislin had mourned her lack of fairy skills. She couldn't turn tiny on her own, sprout wings, fly, talk to animals, or do any of the dozens of other things that she wished she could do. Fairies had used shrinking dust on her a few times before, but it was something she would never get used to. She gulped and tried not to think about her stomach while Peri summoned a dragonfly steed. The dust had worked on both her and Twinket, which gave her mixed feelings. She'd get there faster, but riding a dragonfly made her super sick to her stomach. Darting here and there was not her favorite way to travel.

Peri had a special affinity for dragonflies, however, so they were always his first choice.

Aislin's family always seemed so sure that she'd be thrilled at the chance to fly that she'd never told them how much it bothered her. She'd just have to hope Peri could summon a good tailwind and that the trip wouldn't take too long.

Because Aislin couldn't talk to the dragonfly, she had to depend on Peri to give the insect directions. After the fairy shrank so he was tiny, too, he spoke to the dragonfly for a moment in a buzzing sound, then told Aislin, "His name is Fizzzit. He's flown with me before."

Fizzzit was beautiful with blue and green wings, but he looked grumpy when she climbed on, as if he didn't really want her there. When Peri told the dragonfly to hold still, he did, but the moment she was seated he took off, his wings beating just behind Aislin so she had the wind from the front and the breeze from his wings in the back. She was chilled to the bone within seconds.

"This is fun!" Twinket cried as they left Deephold and darted over the river and the forest canopy.

"Yeah, loads of fun," Aislin said, shivering.

"We're in a real hurry," said Peri, "so I brought some special dust that will help us get there faster."

Opening a second pouch, he took out a pinch of orange fairy dust. It floated over to the dragonfly despite the wind and settled on the insect's head. Although Fizzzit's wings didn't move any faster, he was suddenly speeding through the air. Peri flew beside them as they passed over miles and miles of forest, his own dragonfly-like wings almost a blur. After a while, Aislin was so enthralled by the scenery zipping past below them that she stopped paying attention to her upset stomach.

"Wow!" Twinket exclaimed, grinning from ear to ear. "I've never gone this fast before. Look, I can already see Fairengar."

Aislin looked where the doll was pointing. She was surprised to see that the fairy palace lay straight ahead now, glittering in the light of the setting sun. Made of marble and crystal, moonbeams and sunbeams, the palace was something that only the king and queen of the fairies could have created. Nearly everyone thought it was the most beautiful building in the world. Although Aislin had stayed there many times, she always felt a prickle of excitement when she saw it.

Within minutes, Fizzzit was landing on the palace steps with Peri still beside him. Aislin slid off the dragonfly's back and staggered as the insect flew away. The world seemed to be moving under her feet and the feeling only grew worse when Peri returned her to her normal size. The moment Peri was big again, he hurried off to his next assignment, leaving the princess behind.

Though Aislin was happy to have arrived, she could no longer ignore her queasiness. "I don't feel very well," she told Twinket.

"Then put me down!" Twinket demanded. "If you're going to be sick, don't do it on me." They had traveled together so often that the doll knew the kind of effect that flying had on Aislin.

"I wasn't going to," Aislin replied as she set Twinket on the marble step. "At least, I don't think I was."

When she was in the air, Aislin didn't usually have rock nearby that she could draw on for power. She supposed she could have opened her knapsack to touch the calcite globe, but holding on to the dragonfly had been the most that she could manage. There was plenty of stone in the palace, however, so there was no need to suffer any longer. Taking a seat beside

Twinket, Aislin closed her eyes and reached into the marble. Her body was humming with power when she tapped into her healing abilities to soothe her upset stomach.

Aislin hadn't been sitting there long when Lady Hyacinth appeared at the top of the wide staircase. Lady Hyacinth was one of the fairy queen's ladies-in-waiting and always wore a dress of deep-blue petals. She normally looked very regal and reserved, but when she saw Aislin her eyes lit up and she ran down the steps. Like many fairies, she had never had any children of her own and had been delighted to watch over the infant Aislin. She was still very fond of Aislin, who was just as fond of her.

"My dear, you're here! Queen Surinen told me that you'd be coming and asked me to look out for you, but I didn't know that you'd get here so soon."

"Peri brought me," Aislin told her.

The princess glanced down and spotted some of the orange fairy dust on her shoulder. Wearing a look of distaste, she flicked it off onto the floor.

"You're shivering! That rascal must not have used a warming spell or protected you from the wind. I'll have a word with him later! But let's get you to Her

Majesty's solar and I'll send for a hot drink that will warm you up."

"No, thank you," said Aislin. "I don't think I could drink it right now. My stomach is still a bit off."

"All right. We must hurry though. Your entire family is waiting for you."

Lady Hyacinth chattered the whole way up the gleaming palace steps and along the corridor to the staircase that would take them to the royal chambers. Aislin glanced back now and then to make sure that Twinket was able to keep pace, but the little doll was always right behind her. They were nearing the next staircase when Aislin saw her other best friend, Poppy, coming toward her.

"I have to talk to you," the fairy girl said as she gave Aislin a quick hug hello. "Something has come up and it's super important."

Aislin gave Poppy a closer look, but her friend seemed more excited than nervous or worried. Whatever she wanted to talk about, it had to be something good.

"You'll have to discuss it later," Lady Hyacinth told the girls. "Queen Surinen is expecting the princess."

"I'll talk to you as soon as I can," Aislin told Poppy. "Wait for me in my room."

"Fine, but don't make any decisions without talking to me!" Poppy called as Aislin and Lady Hyacinth hurried up the stairs.

When Aislin glanced back, Twinket had stayed behind to talk to Poppy. Whatever they were discussing, they both seemed very excited.

Aislin was happy to see her family seated in a circle before the huge window that made up one wall of Queen Surinen's solar, but even more interested in what she saw outside the window. Unlike her mother's solar, which was bright and cheerful only when it was sunny out, the fairy queen's solar was always filled with light. Powerful fairy magic made the scenery outside the window change with the queen's whims. Occasionally the window looked out on the forest that actually surrounded the palace. On other days, the view might be of distant mountains or faraway forests. Today a large lake with tall trees rimming it filled the view.

Aislin had gotten only a quick glimpse of the lake when Timzy threw himself at her, almost knocking her to the floor. Aislin hadn't seen her little brother since the human king, Tyburr, took her from Eliasind.

Once she was safely back in the land between the mountains, she had been too busy to go to Eliasind.

"Are you really all right?" Timzy demanded, hugging her like their lives depended on it. "Were the humans horrible to you? Did they hurt you? Because if they did, I'll hunt them down and—"

"They didn't hurt me," Aislin said, kissing the top of his head. "I'm fine. Are you all right?"

"Of course, I am," he said, looking up at her, but his eyes were rimmed with red and she wondered if he'd been crying.

"Let your sister breathe," Queen Maylin said, coming to stand beside them. She patted her son's back, then turned to hug Aislin.

A few seconds later, Aislin's fairy grandmother stepped up, with her arms open. Although Aislin had more pedrasi abilities than fairy, she and Queen Surinen had always had a special bond. They seemed to understand each other without saying a word, and they had the same sense of humor, laughing at things that other people often didn't understand. They also resembled each other, with their dark hair and violet eyes, though the fairy queen's face was more slender and her ears were more pointed. Aislin's pedrasi skin was darker, having tanned from years spent outside. Her pedrasi blood made her sturdier, too. She wasn't a mirror image of her grandmother, but the resemblance was enough that everyone saw it.

"How was your visit with King Talus?" the fairy queen asked as Aislin gave her a hug and kiss on the cheek. Although Aislin treated Queen Surinen with the respect due to the queen when they were in public, she treated her like her grandmother when there was only family around.

"It was good," Aislin said as she went to hug her grandfather. "I met some interesting people and learned some interesting things."

"Did you learn anything more about your abilities?" asked King Darinar.

Aislin nodded. "I did. It seems they're still developing. You'd be surprised by what I can do now."

"We were already surprised," her father told her from across the room. "You'll have to give us a demonstration sometime."

Aislin hurried to greet him. "I will, although I think I'll need a lot of rock around to do it."

Her father looked proud as he reached out to hug her.

"You should have seen what our Aislin did when we were subduing Aghamonda," the fairy king told his wife.

"As you've said a hundred times," she said, smiling gently. Turning to Aislin, she added, "Your grandfather and your father are both very proud of you. You've surpassed all their expectations."

Aislin laughed. "Mine, too."

"Just wait until I'm big like Aislin," Timzy declared. "I'll be able to do all sorts of super things!"

"I'm sure you will," Aislin said, grinning at him. "I expect you'll do a lot of things that I can't."

"We finally made our decision about Aghamonda," Queen Surinen told Aislin as the princess took a seat in the circle.

The fairy Aghamonda had stayed in the human world when most of the other fey had gone to the land between the mountains. While living among the humans, she had become embroiled in their wars, which was against fey law and was the very thing King Darinar had wanted to avoid. After meeting Aislin, the fairy had tried to imprison her beneath the castle in Scarmander. Aislin's father and grandfather had returned to the human world where Aislin had helped them capture Aghamonda. The princess really didn't like the fairy and had been happy to bring her back to Fairengar for sentencing.

"After much deliberation, we've sentenced her to three hundred years in the courtyard as a statue," said the queen. "If she isn't repentant then, she'll receive another three hundred years."

"That sounds about right to me," Aislin told her.

"If we ever let her go free, we'll still place restraints on her," said King Darinar. "Powerful fairies who abuse their power for their own ends are never to be trusted. Once, long ago, we were foolish enough to believe someone like her had become good again and have regretted it ever since."

"Did you ever find out why Aghamonda wanted to trap Baibre in the locket?" Aislin asked.

"We did indeed," her grandfather replied. "Aghamonda had discovered some of the older, long-forbidden magic, including a spell that would transfer another fairy's power to her. The spell was strongest if the fairy was a close relative."

"And so she chose her sister," said Aislin. "How is Baibre now?"

"She's doing very well," said Queen Surinen. "We

helped her find her parents, and they're still here in the palace. If you run into her in the corridors, don't be surprised if you don't recognize her. Baibre's mother convinced her to make herself look young again. I'm not sure how long they'll stay with us, though. Baibre has been talking about taking her parents to live in the human part of the world when we move back."

"When will that be?" Aislin asked her.

"In less than a week," Queen Surinen replied.

Aislin's eyes opened wide in surprise. She hadn't expected it to be nearly that soon.

"We want you to go with us and spend some time in the human world. We've discussed this with your parents and they've given their approval. You already know some of these people and how to deal with them. We thought that having you there might make the transition easier. You can locate the fairies that you met and bring them to court, as well as find others who were left behind who need to be helped. What do you think? Are you interested?"

Aislin didn't have to think about it for long. She had returned from the human world only a week before. It had never occurred to her to go back there so soon, but of course she would go if they needed her. When she nodded, a kind of tenseness left her grandparents' faces and they both smiled. Apparently, they hadn't been so sure that she would say yes.

"Wonderful!" said the king.

"We'll be with you for the move," said Aislin's mother, "but we won't stay for long. As soon as everyone is settled, your father and Timzy and I will go back to Eliasind."

"And that brings me to the reason we wanted you back here now," Queen Surinen told Aislin.

The queen studied her granddaughter's face intently, waiting to see how she'd react as she continued. "Humans will be coming to visit us at court, and you'll be meeting them when you're out and around in their world. We recall from when we lived among them long ago that they were easily impressed with luxury and pretentiousness, as well as shows of strength. It is a common practice among them for queens and princesses to have ladies-in-waiting in attendance. I believe that you will need some as well, if only to keep up appearances."

"But I don't need ladies-in-waiting! I like doing things for myself," said Aislin.

Though she had thought that helping her fairy grandparents would be exciting, she dreaded the thought of dealing with all the rules and protocol of formal palace life.

"I understand that," said the fairy queen. "And in private you need not have them do anything. But when you are in public, you should have your ladies in attendance at all times, just as I do."

"Do you have your ladies-in-waiting just to impress people?" Aislin asked her.

The queen laughed. "I had them when we lived among the humans for that very reason. Later, I'd become so accustomed to having them around, and they'd become so used to the luxurious lives they enjoy in the palace, that I never wanted to make them leave. I'll let you in on a little secret," she said, lowering her voice to a half whisper, "I like doing many things for myself, too."

Aislin smiled back at her and they both laughed. But then it occurred to the princess that she didn't know anything about ladies-in-waiting. "How do I find them? If we're leaving in less than a week, I don't have much time."

"I've made a list of suggestions," Queen Surinen

said. With a wave of her hand, a leaf appeared out of the air and floated down onto Aislin's lap. "You may follow the suggestions or come up with your own list. The choice of who your ladies will be is up to you. All I ask is that you have at least five before we leave. You'll also have fairy guards to watch over you, but I'll take care of assigning them."

Aislin stifled a yawn. "I've had a really long day and I think I need to go to bed before I fall asleep here."

"You must eat first!" cried her grandmother. The queen picked up a bluebell blossom from the table beside her and rang it. A moment later three footmen entered the room carrying platters of fruit, nuts, and small seed cakes.

Aislin glanced out the window, then turned back to her grandmother as the footmen began offering food. "I wanted to ask you about that lake," Aislin said, gesturing toward the window and the glistening water beyond. "I think I'm familiar with all the big lakes in the land between the mountains, but I've never seen that one. What lake is that?"

"It isn't in the land between the mountains," said King Darinar. "That lake is in the human kingdoms, deep in the forest between Scarmander and Tamweld. Before we moved our palace here, we placed a spell on the forest to keep humans out and the land unclaimed in case we ever wanted to return. That lake is where our palace used to be. We filled it with water so nothing would grow there. Now that we're returning, that is where our palace will go."

"The forest is lovely," said Aislin.

"Yes," Queen Surinen replied, "but not nearly as lovely as it will be after we bring magic back to the human kingdoms."

Aislin was struggling to keep her eyes open by the time the family finished their simple meal. Her mother and Timzy escorted her to her suite of rooms and said good night at the door. She went inside, yawning broadly.

Stepping into her suite in the fairy palace was like stepping into another world. Giant toadstools grew up from the mossy floor providing seats around the sitting room. Large windows framed with flowers looked out over the forest where bats were carrying tiny fairies out for an evening ride. A desk shaped from a living tree held a stack of leaves and ink sticks for writing. A fairy light glowed over the desk while others were scattered around the room.

Aislin took off her shoes so she could feel the moss under her feet, but had only a moment to enjoy it before Twinket jumped off a toadstool and came running over. "What took so long? We've been waiting for ages!"

"It wasn't really that long," Poppy said from over by the window. "It just felt like it to us because we want to talk to her about something really, really important."

Aislin sighed and sat down on a toadstool. "All right, what is it that's so terribly important?" she asked. All she wanted to do was go to bed, but she couldn't put her friends off any longer.

"I've heard rumors that Queen Surinen wants you to choose some ladies-in-waiting," said Poppy. "I know for a fact that all the fairy girls are planning to ambush you tomorrow to ask you to pick them and I wanted to tell you that I want to be on that list, too."

"And me!" cried Twinket. "I really, really, really want you to pick me!"

"It's true that I'm supposed to name some girls,

but how did you know about it?" asked Aislin. "I just found out about it myself."

Poppy laughed. "Are you kidding me? This is the fairy queen's palace. It's loaded with fairies who have nothing better to do than use their magic to snoop and be nosy. I could sneeze once in my bedchamber tonight and even the scullery maids would know about it by morning. Half the court has spent days talking about who you would choose to be your ladies-in-waiting."

"I don't know who I'll choose yet," said Aislin. "I have to think about it. But right now, I need to go to bed. I'm so tired I can barely move."

"Are you going to fall asleep sitting there like you did at the campfire?" Twinket asked. "Because if you are I can get you a blanket. That's the kind of thing a lady-in-waiting would do for you and I would be a really good one."

Aislin shook her head and stood up. "I'll just go to bed instead. Good night, you two. I'll think about this whole ladies-in-waiting thing in the morning."

"Here, let me get the door," Poppy said, running to open it.

Aislin half stumbled into her bedchamber and

headed to the large flower-draped bed suspended from the ceiling by four thick, strong vines. She was too tired to bother changing into her nightgown and barely made it onto the bed before she fell asleep.

Aislin woke a few hours later with the light of the full moon filling her room. Rolling onto her side to face away from the window, she pulled the duckling-down comforter over her head to block out the light. Going back to sleep wasn't easy. First, she noticed that she was tucked under the covers, even though she had fallen asleep on top of them. Then, she realized that she was wearing her nightgown, which meant that Poppy had used magic to change her clothes. When she rolled over again, she noticed that Twinket was curled up on the pillow beside her, sound asleep, just as she was most nights in case the princess needed something.

Aislin smiled. Her two closest friends had started acting as her ladies-in-waiting when they went with her to the human lands and had never stopped. She'd start writing her list in the morning. Poppy would be at the head. Aislin would like to put Twinket down, too, but she didn't know how impressed humans would be to see a lady-in-waiting who was a doll, albeit one that could walk and talk. Though, while she once would have hidden Twinket, she no longer had to hide any magic from the humans. Twinket could certainly be an honorary lady-in-waiting.

As for the others... Aislin didn't want ladies-in-waiting like the girls who surrounded the human princess, Selene. Rude and unkind, they were simply the pretty daughters of Selene's stepmother's friends, not people the princess would have picked herself. No, Aislin wanted to choose girls she liked and admired. They didn't need to be pretty. They needed to be girls whom she could depend on, who wouldn't be afraid to do what she needed them to do or go where she had to go. If Aislin was going out into the human kingdoms, she would need girls she could rely on to help her as much as Poppy and Twinket. There was no telling what she might run into when humans were in charge and the fey were only just getting used to being back among them.

And then there were the guards that her grandmother had mentioned. She didn't like the idea of fairy knights following her around wherever she went.

But then maybe she wouldn't need them. If she was smart, she could collect two birds in one basket. Aislin smiled a small, secret smile. She already had a good idea who might qualify to go on her list.

Chapter 7

COOING DOVES WOKE AISLIN the next morning. "Please be quiet," she mumbled, opening her eyes just enough to glance at the birds on her window ledge. The doves grew silent and hunched down into their feathers. Aislin sighed. The birds had only been doing their jobs; it wasn't their fault that she hadn't canceled her normal wake-up coo.

When Aislin looked around, she noticed Twinket was no longer on the other pillow. The princess wondered where the doll had gone, because they usually got up at the same time.

It took Aislin a moment to remember the list she had to write, but then it was all she could think about.

Slipping off the edge of her bed-swing, she padded into the bathing room. A two-foot-high waterfall splashed into the small pond at its base. Dogwood trees that never stopped blooming grew behind the waterfall, while daffodils and crocuses decorated the edge of the pond.

Draping her nightgown over a branch, Aislin stepped into the pool and sank back so that her head was resting on a moss-covered rock that was shaped just for her. Closing her eyes, she thought about whom she would put on the list. Poppy, of course, but she would be the only fairy. A varied group would be more helpful, with their different attributes complementing each other's abilities.

Two girls came to mind immediately, though she knew they would be highly unconventional. Lin was a warrior through and through. As far as Aislin knew, the pedrasi girl had little knowledge of life at the fairy court, but she did know things that could come in handy outside the palace. Like all pedrasi, she had an affinity for rock and could sense her way through mountains—although not as well as Aislin—but it was always good to have a backup. Lin was a warrior, too, and would do well as one of Aislin's guards.

Deela probably didn't know much about the court either, but the orc girl's presence there would be so distracting that people wouldn't notice if she didn't use the correct fork to eat her food. That tendency to distract might come in handy at times. Orcs weren't afraid of anything, which meant that Aislin could send her places that others might fear to go. And as a highly trained fighter, Deela could also count as one of her guards. Orc females were also known to be fiercer than males. Aislin was sure that her grandmother would approve the choice.

Aislin decided that if she was going with unconventional, she might as well include Kimble, the spriggan girl who had shown herself to be brave and resourceful in Mount Gora. She was clever, too, which could definitely come in handy. Kimble would enjoy visiting the fairy court, even if it wasn't Deephold.

That left one more position to fill. Aislin laughed out loud when she thought about whom she'd like to add to the list. The girl was the same age as Deela, but much, much bigger, and would have an even bigger impact at court. Salianne was a giant and one of Aislin's good friends, though they never saw each other as much as they'd like. She was loyal, honest, and caring, all traits that earned Aislin's respect. Her parents were shy, like most giants, and they rarely came to court except when summoned. Aislin had a feeling that Salianne would enjoy the chance to meet people and would make a good addition to the list, regardless of what others might think. If Aislin's ladies-in-waiting were meant to impress the humans, then who better than a giant? And even if she wasn't trained as a warrior, her strength alone would make her an asset as a guard.

Aislin frowned. If her friends were going to be both her ladies-in-waiting and her guards, they needed a new name. She thought about a few, quickly discarding each one. *They're going to be my champions,* she finally mused, *so why not call them that?* The pedrasi word for champion was "mestari," a word she'd always liked. Satisfied with her choices, Aislin reached for her violet-scented soap and scrubbed her arms, washing off the stone dust and grime from her trip. She was working up a good lather when the door to the bathing room burst open and Peony walked in carrying a tray with a covered dish.

"I brought your breakfast, Your Highness," the fairy said, smiling brightly. She was dressed in her best pink-and-white petal dress with her hair arranged on top of her head, as if she was on her way to a fancy party. "There are honey and seed cakes and fresh berries that I picked for you this morning."

Aislin sank under the water so that only her head was showing. "How thoughtful," she said. "You can leave it on the table in my sitting room."

"I will in a minute," Peony said. "But first I want to tell you what a good lady-in-waiting I would be. I could bring you breakfast like this every morning and carry all your messages and write your letters for you. I have very nice writing, as you can see on this note I left on the tray."

"I'm sure you do," said Aislin. "But I don't want to talk about this right now. I'm taking a bath and I want to be alone."

"I just thought you'd want to know that I'm very interested in the position and—"

"Perhaps I haven't made myself clear enough. Please leave," Aislin said.

"Yes! Yes, of course! We can discuss this later," said Peony. "I'll wait for you in your sitting room."

"I'd rather you didn't," Aislin told her.

"Then I suppose you'll summon me later," the fairy said, still looking hopeful. "I'll just leave this on the table."

Aislin sighed as the door shut behind Peony. She knew the fairy, just as she knew most of the fairies in the palace, but they had never been friends or even all that friendly. Peony had always been more interested in gossip and appearances than in helping people, so they had very little in common. Even if Aislin had wanted more fairies on her list, she wouldn't have chosen Peony.

Aislin washed her hair and was under the waterfall, rinsing it, when Rose walked in carrying a pitcher and a dainty cup. Startled, Aislin came out of the water, spluttering. If the fairy had knocked on the door or announced herself, the princess hadn't heard it. "I brought you berry juice!" the fairy said. "It's a mixture I made myself." With her vivid pink hair and bright pink lips, Rose always attracted attention. She was also more interested in the boy fairies than in being friends with a girl and had never had much time for Aislin.

"I'm taking a bath," Aislin said, her irritation growing. "Please leave."

"But I thought we could talk privately, girl to girl," Rose said, and pouted.

"And I'm telling you, princess to girl who wants to be a lady-in-waiting, get out!"

"Of course. Sorry!" Rose said, making the contents of the pitcher slosh as she hurried out the door.

"For flowers' sake!" Aislin said, reaching for a towel.

But it wasn't over. "Here, let me get that for you," said Apple Blossom, handing her the towel.

Aislin gasped and wrapped the towel around herself. "When did you come in?" she cried.

"While you were under the waterfall. I let Rose go first because I knew she'd mess up. It's obvious that she would make a lousy choice. Too pushy, if you ask me. On the other hand, I would make a wonderful lady-in-waiting. I would—"

"Leave!" Aislin shouted. She had never needed a lock on her bathing room door before this, but she was certainly going to request one now. Of course, fairies could get in anyway, but the smarter ones might take the hint.

"Are you sure I can't get you anything first?" asked Apple Blossom.

Aislin grabbed the soap to throw at her, but the fairy turned small and flew out the window before the princess could take aim.

The princess was fuming when she left the

bathing room. She became even angrier when she stepped into her bedchamber and found two more fairies waiting for her. "Get out!" she said through gritted teeth.

Seeing the look on her face, they became tiny and flew away, although they both left notes about themselves behind. Furious, Aislin got dressed in a hurry. When she remembered the list that her grandmother had given to her, she looked around the room, but the everyday magic that kept her rooms tidy had already cleaned and put away the clothes she'd worn the day before. Wondering where the list might be, she stepped into her sitting room to look for it. Three smiling fairies greeted her. They all fled when she glowered at them.

Aislin thought she might have dropped the list, so she looked for it on the floor and beside the toadstool where she'd been sitting, but it wasn't in either place. When she happened to glance at her desk, she found the list prominently displayed in the middle. The leaf was unfolded, though she was certain that it had been folded when she saw it last. Taking a closer look, she saw that there were at least twenty names on the leaf and all of them were fairies'.

Aislin sat at the desk to read over the list. The names of the fairies who had just visited her were at the top. Aislin couldn't understand why her grandmother had suggested so many. Counting them, she found twenty-two names, with no reasons why she should pick any of them.

Shaking her head, she reached for a fresh leaf. She wrote her own list, making sure to include one or two reasons why she wanted each girl. The fairies who had pestered her weren't going to be happy.

After tucking the leaf into her pocket, Aislin started out the door—and almost ran into Azalea, who was waiting just outside. "I know you're very busy, but I just wanted to give you this," the fairy said, handing Aislin a note. "As you can see from my list of accomplishments, I'd make a wonderful lady-in-waiting." The fairy gave her a big smile while backing up a few feet, then turned to hurry away.

Aislin shook her head. Azalea's name was on the list, too. She wondered why her grandmother had picked such pesky fairies.

The princess had just started down the hall, heading for her grandmother's chambers, when she saw Lady Hyacinth and nodded hello.

"Good morning, Your Highness," said the queen's own lady-in-waiting. "I hope you slept well. Queen Surinen asked me to tell you that she's in the fountain courtyard if you wish to talk to her now."

"Thank you," Aislin said, and turned around. She had just started down the stairs when yet another fairy coming up them stopped right in front of her, blocking her way.

Hydrangea was wearing a soft blue-petalled dress that rustled when she moved. "We need to talk," the fairy told her. "I understand that lots of eligible fairies want to be one of your ladies-in-waiting, but you really need to be careful making your decision. You want someone you can trust. Someone you can rely on."

"I understand that," said Aislin as she stepped to the side, hoping to walk around the fairy.

Hydrangea stepped to the side, too, blocking Aislin again. "A lot of fairies in the castle are gossips. I can give you their names if you'd like. They would never keep your secrets and would tell everyone everything about you."

"That's good to know," Aislin said, and tried to get past her again.

"*I'm* very discreet, however," said Hydrangea.

"And observant. I'm also a good listener. Why, I was just telling my friend Cowslip the other day that I'm the best listener I know."

"I'm sure you are," Aislin replied, "but I need to get past you. If you'll excuse me."

Hydrangea looked surprised. "What? Oh, sure. Just let me know when you want me to start as lady-in-waiting. I'll need a few days to clear my schedule."

When the fairy still didn't move aside, Aislin hurriedly stepped around her and continued down the stairs. She had just reached the first floor when a beautiful fairy with flowing blue hair came running over. "Princess Aislin! May I speak with you for a moment?"

Although Aislin didn't recognize her, there was something familiar about the fairy. "Let me guess— you want to be one of my ladies-in-waiting," Aislin replied.

"Uh, no, not at all," the fairy said, sounding confused. "I just want to thank you for all you've done. I'm Baibre! Remember me? I looked much older the last time we met. You were there when that human boy gave me the necklace and I got pulled into the amber locket. I blamed you and that boy for what happened at first, but I had plenty of time to think and I realized that it wasn't your fault. You couldn't have known what my sister was like or what she had planned. When King Darinar put Aghamonda in the locket with me, I made her tell me what she had been up to and I was appalled! To think you stopped her. Well, I just wanted to thank you for bringing me to Queen Surinen. She straightened everything out and I couldn't be happier."

"I'm glad it all worked out," Aislin told her. "I'm just sorry it happened in the first place and that I wasn't able to get you out of the locket myself."

"Oh, poo. Don't give it another thought. Being stuck in that locket with my sister gave me plenty of time to tell her what I thought of her. She was the only one who really suffered! But I have to say that I'm glad she's a statue now. My sister has always been a vengeful terror, even when she was little. At least now my parents and I will have a few hundred years without having to worry about what Aghamonda might have cooked up."

Aislin was relieved. She had been worried about Baibre and Aghamonda being trapped in the locket together. Although King Darinar had wrapped Aghamonda in vines and put a wad of leaves in her mouth after the battle, Aislin had wondered if the fairy was completely powerless. She'd been afraid for Baibre, though apparently the fairy could handle herself just fine.

Aislin finally found her grandmother in the courtyard, standing in the sunlight examining a life-like statue. Aislin was taken aback when she realized that the statue looked a bit like Baibre...until she remembered that Aghamonda was the fairy's twin. Stepping closer, Aislin touched the statue with a tentative finger. This was stone, but it was also a living being, frozen in time.

"She can't move or speak, but she's aware of what's going on around her and can hear what I'm saying right now," said Queen Surinen. "If she knows what's good for her, she'll repent her ways. If she doesn't, she'll have to get used to standing here forever. I'd feel sorry for her, but she brought this on herself for colluding with humans in a war. Now, tell me, have you given that list any thought?"

Aislin nodded. "I did. A lot of thought, actually, and I came up with a list of my own. I have a question, though. Why did you give me such a big list of names if you wanted me to pick five?"

Queen Surinen frowned. "I gave you a list of seven names. I don't see how that's very big."

Aislin took the fairy queen's leaf out of her pocket and handed it to her. "I was too tired to look at it last night, but when I checked it this morning, I found twenty-two names on your list."

The queen took the leaf from Aislin. "This isn't my list!" cried the queen. "A few of the names were ones I picked, but the rest are fairies that I wouldn't even consider. The handwriting looks like mine though. Just a moment and I'll get to the bottom of this."

With a tap of her finger, Queen Surinen made the leaf turn black. Seven names on the list glowed yellow, while the rest turned blood red. "I see what happened. The fairies whose names are red used magic to add themselves to the list. I didn't know my fairies could be so brazen! I'll have to speak to them about this."

"Here's my list," Aislin said, and took it out of her other pocket. "I'm afraid I didn't use your list at all. I don't intend to sit around writing letters and chatting over tea while ladies wait on me. There are places I need to go and people I need to see. My ladies will have to keep up with what I plan to do, so I don't want the traditional ladies-in-waiting. I thought about the qualities I'd want in a lady-in-waiting and chose from the people I know. As you can see, I've included some who can qualify as my guards as well as my ladies. I came up with a new name for all of them. I'm going to call them my mestari."

"How marvelous!" her grandmother cried. "That's a very good name for them. I knew you'd handle this your own way."

Looking over the list, Queen Surinen nodded as she read Aislin's choices. "Wonderful. I'll inform them right away," she finally said. "I think it's good that you didn't include anyone from my list, considering what happened. I don't believe that the fairies who added their names deserve to be your mestari. They've automatically disqualified themselves. I know they'll be disappointed, but it serves them right for trying to go around me. Besides, not one of them would have been nearly as suitable for what you seem to have in mind as the ladies you've chosen."

Chapter 8

THAT VERY MORNING, QUEEN Surinen held a meeting in the throne room, summoning all the fairy maidens who had wanted to be Aislin's ladies-in-waiting. "I know that there has been much curiosity and debate over who Princess Aislin should choose to be her ladies," said the queen. "Normally I wouldn't make this announcement, but because some fairies have taken it upon themselves to add their names to the list, I feel I must set things straight. Princess Aislin has made her choices and will be delivering her invitations soon."

The ever-hopeful fairies quivered with anticipation as they cast furtive glances at Aislin.

When the queen told them, "Those of you who added your names to the list without my permission have been disqualified, so you need not look for a letter from the princess," more than one fairy started crying and flew away. "From now on, Princess Aislin's ladies-in-waiting will be called her mestari. I hope that all of you will welcome the new mestari and do your best to make them comfortable among us," the queen added.

Queen Surinen had already left the throne room when one fairy asked another, "Does that mean the new mestari don't live here already?"

"I don't know," said the second fairy. "Don't all the best fairies live in the palace?"

Poppy turned to Aislin with a question in her eyes. "I didn't add my name to any list," the fairy said, sounding hopeful.

"You didn't need to," Aislin told her.

Just then a tiny fairy flew up and landed in front of Poppy. Peri grew big long enough to hand her a folded leaf before he nodded and became tiny again. "Is this what I hope it is?" Poppy asked Aislin as Peri flew off.

"Take a look and see," Aislin said.

Opening the leaf, Poppy hurriedly read the message inside and looked up to grin at Aislin.

"That shouldn't be a surprise," Aislin told her. "Did you really think I might not ask you?"

"You asked *her*?" Hydrangea said from only yards away. "That isn't fair!"

"Why not?" Aislin asked, irritated. "Poppy has always been there for me and has helped me whenever I needed it."

"If I'd known that was all it took, I would have done that ages ago," Hydrangea said, looking bitter. "The rumors I heard about you were right. You are a hateful girl."

"What rumors?" Poppy asked, looking puzzled.

"*She* says that the princess doesn't care what anyone else thinks or what would be best for the fey. The princess only thinks about what she wants, which is why we're moving back to the human lands. The princess liked it there, so now we all have to go."

Aislin frowned. "That isn't it at all."

"Who is this 'she' you're talking about?" Poppy demanded.

"Someone I met who opened my eyes to a lot of things," Hydrangea replied. "I guess I shouldn't be surprised that the princess is asking her friends to be her mestari. The rest of us never stood a chance!" Darting a scornful look at Aislin, the fairy made herself small and flew off.

"I don't like to hear that someone is spreading rumors," Aislin said, and looked around as if one of the other fairies might have something to add. "Do any of you know anything about this person?"

Only a few fairies were left. Most of them shook their heads, but two refused to meet her eyes and flew off before Poppy or Aislin could question them.

Disquieted at the thought that someone was spreading nasty rumors about her, Aislin turned to leave the room. The fey had mentioned something similar when she was returning to Deephold from Mount Gora, but the trip to Fairengar had put it out of her mind. Hearing that the rumors had spread this far was even more disconcerting. And as if that wasn't bad enough, now a group of fairies resented her because she hadn't chosen them. Although she couldn't have chosen all of them anyway, and some were bound to be disappointed no matter what, Aislin had a feeling that they were going to resent her actual picks even more when they discovered whom she had chosen to be her mestari.

After spending her life among fairies, Aislin knew that they easily felt slighted and were known to hold grudges. Although she appreciated her grandmother's efforts, she wasn't sure that the fairies would let their rejection go so easily. The only thing that might keep them in line was their fear of what the fairy queen could do if they misbehaved. Queen Surinen was known for being kind and generous to those who deserved it, but she could also be harsh and vengeful when someone was in the wrong.

Aislin wasn't worried that the fairies might take it out on her. First of all, the fairies had watched Aislin grow up and none of them had ever been mean or unkind to her; it would be odd to start now. Secondly, everyone knew that the queen was very protective of her family. Doing anything hurtful to a member of the royal family could make Queen Surinen truly angry. Poppy was a different story, however, and would make an easy target if a fairy wanted to take her disappointment out on anyone. Aislin hoped it wouldn't come to that.

But Aislin had something else to attend to. "I need to see Twinket," Aislin told her friend, and they started toward the princess's rooms.

They found the doll seated on the floor of the

bedchamber, plucking the loose fur off a longhaired cat. "What are you doing?" asked Poppy. "You've got cat fur floating all over the room!"

"Furball is hot and itchy. I'm taking her loose fur to weave into a blanket for Aislin. I thought Poppy could help me with the weaving part," she said, giving the fairy a hopeful look.

"I'm not weaving cat fur!" the fairy replied. "But I will clean up this mess." With a flick of her fingers, the floating fur flew down into the pile on the floor as if a magnet had drawn it there. When the fur was all collected in one place, Poppy gave a satisfied nod and said, "There! I've completed my first task as one of Aislin's mestari!"

Twinket yanked at Furball's fur so hard that the cat hissed and stalked away. "You're a mestari?" the doll asked Poppy. "What about me?"

"That's why we came back to the room," Aislin told her as she handed the doll a leaf. "Here's your letter. It's naming you an honorary mestari."

"Really?" Twinket cried. "That's even better than a regular one! You already know that out of all your mestari, I'll be the very best one. I can't wait to start. What can I do?"

"You could take that cat fur somewhere else," said Aislin. "And promise that if you do turn it into a blanket, that you won't give it to me. I don't want a cat fur blanket."

"Okay," Twinket declared. "In that case, I'll just throw it out. It smells like Furball, anyway."

The doll had gathered up the fur and was carrying it out of the room when two full-sized fairies carrying baskets arrived at the door. Aislin knew Sage and Parsley very well; the two seamstress fairies had made many of her favorite gowns over the years.

"Queen Surinen wants us to make gowns for you and your mestari," Sage said as she set her basket on the table. "That is what you're calling your ladies, isn't it?"

"It is," Aislin said, glancing at Poppy and Twinket. "Mestari have a much more important job than that of a lady-in-waiting."

Poppy grinned and stood a little taller while Twinket stopped in the doorway and turned around, her smile so big that all her seed-pearl-sized teeth showed.

"To show how important they are, I'd like to have a new mestari emblem created that incorporates the fairy leaf and the pedrasi hammer," Aislin told Sage.

"I'd like you to put the emblem on my mestari's clothing."

"We can do that," Sage replied and Parsley nodded.

"I know some of your ladies haven't arrived yet, but we can get started with you, if you don't mind, Your Highness," said Sage. "The queen wants your gowns to be especially beautiful, as they're meant to impress the humans."

"Poppy is one of my ladies," Aislin told them. "You can start hers, too."

"And mine!" Twinket called from the doorway. "I'm a mestari! In fact, I'm an honorable mestari, which means that I'm the best and should go first, right after the princess."

"I thought you were taking care of that cat fur," reminded Poppy.

Twinket nodded vigorously. "I am. I'll be right back!" The doll dashed down the hall, leaving a floating trail of cat fur behind her.

"She meant honorary," Aislin told the seamstresses. "And she can have new gowns, too."

"Very good," Sage said with a smile. When Aislin was just a toddler, Sage and Parsley had helped Queen

Surinen create Twinket, though it was the queen's magic that had brought the doll to life. The two fairies had always been fond of the doll and looked pleased to hear that she had acquired a new job.

"As a fairy princess, you must wear only the best," Sage said as Parsley emptied the baskets onto the table. "We've brought you lots to choose from. Just tell us what kinds of gowns you'd like."

Aislin examined precious goods from all over, brought back by traveling fairies. She saw sea foam and bits of coral from the Misty Sea, pearls from the coast of the Sunny Isles, moonbeams and rainbows collected in Eliasind, diamonds from the land past the mountains, as well as flowers of every kind and color. After much discussion, the two seamstresses used their magic to make her everyday dresses as well as gowns for fancy dress balls.

None of the gowns were ordinary, but the most impressive was the one made of moonbeams. When Aislin protested that she didn't need a gown like that, Sage told her, "I happen to know that you'll need this gown very soon. Your grandmother specifically told us to make it."

"Can you tell me why?" asked Aislin.

The fairy's eyes twinkled when she said, "Some things are meant to be surprises."

Twinket dashed into the room, so excited that she was vibrating. "When will it be my turn?" she asked. "I want lots of dresses!"

"A soon as I fetch some fabric," Parsley replied. Taking a golden needle from her strawberry-shaped pincushion, Parsley blew through the needle's eye. Pink sparkles heralded the arrival of bolts and squares and mounds of fabric more varied than a rainbow.

Twinket's fabric hands made a soft padding sound as she clapped. "They're all so pretty. Can I have one of each?"

"You won't need that many!" Aislin said with a laugh.

"Poppy, I'll help you while Parsley works with Twinket," said Sage. "You'll wear poppy petals, of course. I think we'll include some poppy leaves as well. Do you have any color preferences?"

"Red's my favorite," Poppy told her as she followed the seamstress to the other side of the room to study her choices.

As the morning wore on, Aislin went from one

side of the room to the other, giving her friends her opinion only when asked. The rest of the day went quickly, with a short break for lunch. It was late afternoon when Sage said, "I believe we're done for the day. There are a few last-minute touches that I want to make to the gowns, so I'll bring them all back to you tomorrow."

Before they left, Sage and Parsley used magic to whisk away the nearly finished gowns as well as the leftover bits and pieces. The room was neat and tidy once again when the seamstresses shut the door behind them.

Aislin glanced out the window to check the sun's position in the sky. "It's time to get ready for supper," she told her friends. "I'll see you both later."

She went into her bathing room to freshen up, then put on her sky-blue gown decorated with snowdrop flowers. Twinket climbed onto the window ledge and waved when Poppy came to the door. The two girls walked to the great hall together. Then Poppy left to take her own seat below the dais. Soon after Aislin sat down at her grandparents' table, the king and queen entered and everyone stood. When the queen nodded and they all sat down again, Aislin glanced at the empty chairs where her parents should be sitting. The queen noticed and said, "I believe they're still in the council chamber meeting with some of the fey who will be staying behind when we move the palace. I don't know if we told you, but all the land between the mountains that was part of Fairengar is now going to be part of Eliasind. Your parents' kingdom is more than tripling in size."

"Did my parents know that this was going to happen?" Aislin asked.

"No, although we had discussed the possibility with your grandfather, King Talus," said King Darinar. "He gave the plan his full approval."

Aislin was delighted. Her parents would rule over the land just the way her grandparents had, which meant that everything would stay the same. All the fey who had fretted over the king and queen leaving needn't have worried at all.

"What did you do today, my dear?" the queen asked her.

"I was getting fitted for my new gowns," Aislin replied. "I really don't know why I need so many."

"No one puts a shabby frame on a masterpiece," the queen said. "A fairy princess always needs to look her best, particularly when dealing with humans. Your gowns will be the first thing they notice. Humans rely heavily on first impressions."

"You're right, of course," said Aislin. "I met a lot of humans in Morain who did just that."

"Are your new mestari enjoying their titles?" Queen Surinen asked.

"Oh yes!" said Aislin. "Especially Twinket. She was thrilled to get new dresses. I didn't know she liked new clothes so much or I would have had some made for her long before this."

The queen smiled. "She probably likes clothes because Sage and Parsley each had a hand in her making. Some of their enthusiasm probably passed on to the doll. Tell me, have the fairies who weren't chosen given you any trouble?"

"No," Aislin said, looking out over the assembled fairies eating at the rows of long tables. "Though I can tell they aren't happy about it from the way they look at me."

"They should get over it," the queen said with a shrug. "But let me know if they don't. I know my fairies and what they're capable of doing. Sometimes I have to remind them of their place."

The cook had prepared some new vegetable dishes with sautéed greens and fried tubers, all of which Aislin liked. After supper, a few fairies played the flute, the drums, and a stringed fairy instrument called the bandolino while other fairies danced—some in the air and some on the ground. Aislin enjoyed the entertainment, but by the time it was over she was ready to go to bed.

Twinket was asleep on one of the pillows when Aislin walked into her chamber. Not wanting to wake the doll, she undressed quietly and slipped under the covers. Moments later she was fast asleep as well.

The stars were shining into the window when Twinket poked Aislin's face to wake her. "Deela and Lin just got here," the doll announced. "Peri made them little and found bats for them to ride. The steward was really surprised when he saw that Deela is an orc. He showed them to their rooms and they've gone to bed already. I wanted to tell them that I'm an honorable mestari and better than them, but now they'll have to wait until morning to find out."

"Honorary, not honorable," Aislin murmured

from under the covers. "And no mestari is better than any other."

"You can say that," said Twinket. "You're a princess and better than just about everybody, but I know I'm right."

"I hear you need my help," a soft voice said. Aislin opened her eyes again and looked around. The sun was just starting to come up, fading the black of night to the gray of early morning.

"Who said that?" Aislin asked. When she saw that Twinket was still asleep and she couldn't spot anyone else in the room, she decided that she must have dreamt it.

She had just closed her eyes when the voice said, "I'm down here. I didn't think it would be polite to climb onto your bed uninvited, but I will if you want me to. It won't be easy though—your bed *is* hanging from the ceiling."

Aislin sat up with a start. She'd suddenly recognized the voice and knew just where to look. Peering over the edge of the bed, she saw Kimble, the spriggan girl, gazing up at her.

"I do need you," Aislin said. "I want you to be one of my mestari, if you're interested. You'll be my companion and champion and guard all rolled into one. It's going to be a very prestigious position."

"I wouldn't have come all this way on the back of a wild boar if I wasn't interested," said Kimble.

"You rode a boar?" Twinket asked, making the bed shiver as she stalked across it.

Kimble nodded. "I'm afraid of flying, so that fairy—I think his name was Peri—put out a call for an animal to carry me. A grumpy old boar was the first one to come, so I rode him all the way here."

Twinket leaned over the side of the bed to see her. "That explains why you smell like a pig. You need a bath."

"And you need to learn some manners," Kimble replied. "What are you, anyway? You don't look real."

"I'm real!" Twinket exclaimed. "I'm a real living doll. And you're a spriggan. I've seen your kind in Deephold when I've visited with Aislin."

The little spriggan girl yawned and looked around. "I really need to sleep. I've been up all night holding onto that boar's stinky bristles. Are we all sleeping in here or do I get a room, too?"

"You get your own room," Aislin hurried to say. "And welcome to Fairengar," she added as an afterthought.

"Fairengar, huh? It sounds like someplace fairies would live." Kimble smacked her palm against the side of her head. "Oh, right—it is. I really need some sleep."

Chapter 9

KIMBLE WAS STILL IN Aislin's room when a heart-stopping roar shattered the early morning quiet. "What was that?" the spriggan girl asked, her hand going to a dagger on her belt.

"That was an angry orc," Twinket explained. "And since there's only one orc in the palace right now, I'd say that had to be Deela."

Aislin shoved her feet into her slippers as she said, "We need to go see what's wrong."

"Who is Deela?" Kimble asked.

"Another one of my mestari," Aislin told her. "I guess you're about to get your introduction."

Aislin led the way to the hall with the two

little girls hurrying behind her. When she opened the door, she heard angry voices shouting just a few doors away.

"I'll rip your head off if you don't undo that right now!" bellowed the orc.

"I'm not undoing anything!" a fairy screamed back. "Let me go!"

Following the voices, Aislin ran to the third door down the hall and threw it open. The orc girl was standing in the middle of the room holding a hairbrush in one hand and a tiny fairy in the other. From the shock of blue hair that she could see, Aislin guessed that the furious fairy was Hydrangea. The rest of her, including her wings and arms, was trapped inside Deela's hand.

"What is going on?" Aislin demanded as Poppy and Lin ran into the room. Poppy was wearing an ugly mud-colored nightgown that made Lin stop and look at her.

"This *creature* snatched me out of the air and won't let me go!" Hydrangea cried as she struggled to get free.

"I caught this pipsqueak putting nettles in my hairbrush," Deela said, glaring at the fairy. "I just got here and she's already playing tricks on me. I don't even know her!"

Two fairy guards flew into the room and turned big as soon as they landed.

"I've got this handled," Aislin told them. "I think I know what's going on here. Deela, please put Hydrangea down. She's not going anywhere right now."

Deela brought the fairy close to her face and growled, "This isn't over yet. You'd better not leave until the princess says you can go." Grunting, she set the fairy on the floor.

A moment later, Hydrangea was full-sized and so angry that her face was red. "How dare you treat me like that, you … you orc!"

"Let me see that brush," Aislin said, holding out her hand. The brush was full of nettles that would snag the hair of anyone who tried to use it. When she turned to Hydrangea, she saw a bulge in the fairy's pocket and some nettles stuck to the outside. "Why did you do this?" she asked the fairy.

"Because you made her one of your ladies-in-waiting!" the fairy blurted out. "That job should have been mine, not some horrible orc with fangs and talons who smells like a bat."

Deela snarled, showing off her sharply pointed fangs. Her eyes glinted red as she glared at Hydrangea. The fairy shrank back, her face turning pale.

"They're called mestari now, and the ladies I chose were the most qualified," said Aislin. "As such, they deserve your respect. If anyone is rude or unkind to them, that fairy will have to answer to me. Do you understand what I'm saying?"

Hydrangea nodded, although she didn't look happy about it.

"Lin and I were on patrol," Deela told them. "When we got back, a fairy was waiting for us and he said we had to come right away. He made us small and summoned bats for us to ride. I was too tired to take a bath once we got here."

"Did Hydrangea do anything to you?" Aislin asked as she turned to Lin.

The pedrasi girl shrugged. "I don't know if it was her, but somebody put gravel in my bed."

"What about you, Poppy?" Aislin said, turning to her friend.

"I wasn't going to tell you, because I wanted to deal with it myself," said Poppy, "but when I got back to my room after the fittings, someone had turned all my clothes the color of mud and put snail slime in my shoes."

Aislin turned to Hydrangea and frowned. "Did you do that, too?"

"No," the fairy said, looking surly.

"Do you know who did?" asked Aislin.

The fairy shook her head.

"Then it was probably another fairy I turned down," said Aislin. "Maybe more than one. Didn't any of you hear Queen Surinen say that she wanted you to help my mestari feel welcome and comfortable here? Did you think that was just a suggestion?"

"Uh, no?" Hydrangea said as if she wasn't sure of the answer.

"I want you to remove all the nettles you put in this brush. Make it even cleaner than it was before. Queen Surinen wants me to tell her if any fairies do anything unkind to my ladies. I think this qualifies. Return to your room and stay there until Queen Surinen sends for you. Do you understand that I've just given you an order, not a suggestion?"

Hydrangea's face had gone pale when she said, "Yes, Your Highness."

"Deela, make sure there's nothing in your bed,

then get some sleep," Aislin told her. "That goes for the rest of my ladies, too. You all have a busy day ahead of you and I want you well rested. Once the palace moves, you might not get the chance to sleep in again for a long time."

Although Aislin would have loved to go back to bed, she already had too many things to do. She knew that Queen Surinen was an early riser, and that the news of what had happened would spread. If Aislin didn't hurry, she wouldn't be the first to tell the queen. Not wanting her grandmother to get a slanted version of the story, Aislin returned to her rooms and dressed as quickly as she could. She found her grandmother in her chambers sipping dandelion tea from a tulip cup.

"Good morning," said the queen. "I hear you've had some excitement today. My guards were already here. They told me what they'd seen."

"It wasn't the kind of excitement we need," Aislin replied. "It seems that some of your fairies are ready to take out their feelings on my mestari after all."

"What do you think we should do about it?" asked Queen Surinen. "I could remove their ability to fly for a month, or ban them from the festivities we have planned."

"I thought about it on my way here," said Aislin. "Instead of punishing them, maybe we should get them to help. Peri has been awfully busy bringing people to the palace, so I doubt he's been able to notify everyone about the move. I'm sure there are still fey who don't know that you're returning to the human lands. We want everyone to know about the move, even in the farthest reaches of the land between the mountains, so everyone can decide if they want to stay here or go. We don't want anyone to be left behind by mistake, like what happened the last time the palace moved. I think we should tell the fairies that we need them to go out as temporary messengers to spread the word. They won't have the time or the energy to get into trouble if they're doing something useful."

"That's a marvelous idea!" said the queen. "I already have other messengers notifying the fey in the forest, but we could certainly use the help. I suspect that some of the fairies you turned down have gotten rather lazy and thought that being one of your ladies-in-waiting would give them power and prestige without doing much work. It's time they made themselves useful, so I'll give them a choice. They either volunteer to help, or they can stay here and be grounded for a month."

Aislin smiled. "I'd be surprised if they thought that was a real choice."

Once again Queen Surinen summoned the fairies who had put their names on the list. When they were all assembled, she told them that she held them all responsible for the tricks played on the mestari. After giving them the choices she'd discussed with Aislin, she added, "Those of you who harass any of Princess Aislin's mestari from this time on will be banished from court and unable to return for one hundred years."

The fairies had been casting furtive glances at each other, but they all gasped and stared at the queen when she mentioned banishment. Aislin well knew that the fairies who lived at the palace loved the luxury and excitement of the fairy court and that none of them would want to risk that. She wasn't at all surprised when the fairies flocked to volunteer.

With only a few days before the fairy palace returned to the human world, everyone was busy. The new fairy messengers flew off right away while the fey who had decided to stay in the land between the mountains said goodbye to their friends and left the palace with their possessions. The fey who lived in the forest and wanted to return to the human lands came to the palace where they would stay until after the move. All the fey who took care of the palace and those who lived in it dashed around, seeing that no one forgot anything when they left and that all the new arrivals had rooms to stay in and everything they needed. It helped that magic kept the rooms clean, but magic didn't keep fey from getting lost in the vast palace or struggling to find seats in the great hall for supper.

Aislin let her newly arrived mestari sleep in, but by midday Sage and Parsley were eager to get started on their gowns. Lin was the first one up, so they started on hers. An hour later they were working on gowns for Deela as well. When Aislin went to check on them, she found that the pedrasi girl was upset.

"We can't fight in these things!" Lin cried, holding out the skirt of a green gown that matched her eyes. "I don't mind dressing up to help you, but not in something that makes it hard to run or wield my hammer." She pointed to the war hammer leaning up against the wall. Like all pedrasi weapons, it was weighted for battle and looked quite formidable.

"The same goes for me," said Deela, who had heard them from an adjoining room. She stuck her head in the door and scowled. "We're fighters, not bits of fluff who sit around looking pretty. Your seamstresses can make our clothes look nice, but they have to give us freedom to move and do what we need to do."

The princess nodded. "You're right. I didn't think of that. Can you manage to make what they want?" she asked Sage.

"Well, yes. I suppose," the fairy replied. "I know the kinds of things your ladies like now. Let Parsley and me see what we can do."

"Good," said Aislin. "Then come with me, ladies. I want to introduce you to some people. Has anyone seen Kimble?"

"We did her gowns this morning," Parsley told her. "She said that she never sleeps for long and was up and about hours ago. The last we saw of her, she was going somewhere with Twinket."

Aislin grinned. "Then she's in good hands. I'm sure Twinket will show her things that would never occur to me to put on my tour."

Poppy joined Aislin, Lin, and Deela when they passed her rooms. The four of them were old friends and had lots to discuss. However, as they approached the royal suites and saw the guards in the hallway, the two new arrivals grew quiet. When Queen Surinen bade them enter, both Lin and Deela seemed nervous, especially when they saw that the king was there talking to his wife.

"Your Majesties," Aislin began, "I'd like to introduce two of my new ladies-in-waiting to you. Tourmaline and Deela have both been guards in Deephold. I've known them for many years and have found them to be honest and trustworthy."

"Welcome to Fairengar," Queen Surinen said, smiling gently. It was part of the fairy queen's magic to be able to terrify visitors or put them at ease when she willed it. Both Lin and Deela relaxed and smiled back.

"We're pleased that our granddaughter made such good choices for her ladies-in-waiting," the queen told them. "I'm sure you will help her in whatever capacity she needs."

"We intend to," Lin said, patting the place where her war hammer usually hung from her belt, forgetting that it wasn't there.

The king noticed her gesture. When he glanced at the queen, she nodded.

"I'm about to show Lin and Deela around the palace," Aislin told her grandparents.

"We were just going to send for you," said the king. "Perhaps Poppy can take them instead."

"I'd be happy to show them around," Poppy said. "Your Majesties." She bowed before backing out of the room with Lin and Deela following her example.

"You received a note from Salianne's parents," Queen Surinen told Aislin, gesturing to a huge leaf draped over a nearby table. "It seems that they appreciate the honor of the offer, but feel that their daughter isn't old enough for such a task. How old did you say she is?"

"She's sixteen," Aislin replied. "I'm sorry they feel that way. It really is too bad, because I think Salianne would have liked to come, but her parents have always been strict."

"I'd prefer that giant parents are strict with their children rather than letting them run wild," said the king. "Undisciplined giants often get into trouble."

"There was something else we wanted to discuss," Queen Surinen said. "We'll be moving the palace tomorrow. When we do, we'll need your help and that of your parents. We moved it to the land between the mountains without anyone's assistance, but we think that everything will go much more smoothly with your added magic."

"I don't know what I could do," said Aislin.

"Your being here will be enough," the king replied. "Queen Surinen and I will handle everything."

The night before the move, Aislin was too excited to get much sleep. It was still dark out when she climbed out of bed and got dressed. She was supposed to eat breakfast in Queen Surinen's chambers with her family, so she hurried down the hallway, certain that her grandparents would be up getting ready.

Everyone but Timzy was already there, eating nut and seed cakes, and drinking juice from tulip cups. When they had all finished, Queen Surinen said, "It's time for us to begin. All we need you to do is stand behind us and set your hands on our shoulders. We can draw magical strength from you when we need it.

Don't budge once we get started. The move itself won't take long."

King Darinar and his queen sat in two chairs facing the window and reached for each other's hands. Aislin's parents took their places behind the chairs, leaving room for the princess to stand between them. All three set one hand on Queen Surinen's shoulder and one on King Darinar's. Nothing seemed to happen at first. While she waited, Aislin glanced out the window at the forest and could see that the sun was just starting to come up. The colors were vibrant, and the dew on the leaves sparkled with silver and gold flecks. Suddenly Aislin's fingers began to tingle and she felt a weird thrumming running through her. The palace seemed to shift beneath her feet as the view through the window became gray and fuzzy. A sound like rushing water filled the air. Bright streaks of light shot past the window and the entire palace began to shake. There was a sensation of movement, a small bump, and the sound stopped. Once again Aislin could see a forest outside the window, but this forest was duller with muted colors and no sparkle or shine. She remembered how dull the human world had looked during her last visit and knew that they had arrived.

Within moments of setting down, the doors to the palace opened and the fey darted out to explore. Aislin was still looking out the window when she saw the colors begin to brighten and streaks of light trace designs in the shadows of the forest as the fairies exulted in their arrival. Magic had returned to the human world. Anything could happen now.

Chapter 10

"ARE YOU READY TO go, Father?" King Carrigan asked King Darinar.

"Where are you going?" Aislin asked them.

"To open the Magic Gate," King Darinar told her. "We never intended to keep it closed forever."

"But we won't be leaving it unguarded," her father assured Aislin. "Two magic guardians will watch over the pass. Only those with good intentions will be allowed to enter the land between the mountains."

"They'll be back soon," Queen Surinen said. "Your grandfather and I still have much to do here."

Aislin wasn't sure she liked the idea that humans would be able to freely enter the land between the mountains. Good intentions were one thing, but what would the humans actually *do*? When the two fairy men left the room, Aislin turned to her mother. "They're going to let humans in? Is Father really going to trust what they say? You know that humans often lie."

"We know," said Queen Maylin. "Which is why we're going to have the magic guardians alert us when any humans pass through the gate. We're also going to tell the animals and birds of the forest to follow anyone who enters Eliasind. We've grown more cautious after what happened to you. Your father has already used his magic to make our castle impenetrable. No unwelcome visitors will ever be able to enter again."

"Why don't you and your ladies-in-waiting go outside to look around?" Queen Surinen suggested to Aislin. "A great deal will be going on outside right now. It's a very exciting time to be here."

"I'd like that," Aislin said. After kissing her mother and her grandmother, she hurried to her rooms to get ready, sending word to her ladies on the way.

Aislin decided to try on the special clothes that Sage and Parsley had made. The fairy seamstresses had designed the clothes that Lin and Deela had wanted, then had gone a step further and made them for the other girls as well. Not only were the leather tunics and leggings pretty with embroidered vines and leaves, they all bore the mestari emblem that Aislin had wanted and were flexible enough to satisfy even the pedrasi and orc girls.

Twinket was excited to hear that she now had a reason to wear her "fun clothes," as she called the tunic and leggings. Aislin thought the doll looked very cute in them; Twinket thought so, too.

"Maybe I should wear these all the time," the doll said as the other ladies joined them.

"And not wear those fancy gowns Parsley made for you?" said Poppy. "Give it some time and you'll have a chance to wear all your new clothes."

Twinket looked very pleased.

When they reached the first floor of the palace, they found a throng of fey heading toward the main entrance. Aislin's mestari gathered around her, escorting her through the crowd and out the door. The princess couldn't help but pause when she reached the top step. The palace had settled in the center of a large lake with sandy beaches and the forest just beyond. It was a beautiful setting and was becoming even lovelier as the fey used their magic. Color exploded at the edge of the forest where a group of fairies danced. The leaves became a lusher green, and the wild flowers spread even as Aislin watched.

A wide bridge made of the clearest crystal arched over the water, connecting the palace to the shore. As Aislin and her mestari stepped onto the bridge, she looked down and saw nymphs splashing in the lake below. One group was racing through the water, disappearing around the side of the palace. The water itself seemed to be clearer and less murky the longer the nymphs played in it.

Other fey had followed the princess's group outside. Seeing the lake, three water nymphs cried out in delight and dove off the bridge, plunging into the water to swim just below the surface. When fairies spotted the group dancing in the forest, they became tiny and flew off to join their friends.

"Look at that!" Twinket cried. Aislin glanced at the doll and saw that she was sprawled face down on the bridge, peering through the crystal. "Those nymphs are tickling the fish!"

"What fun!" cried Kimble. "I wish I could do that. Let's go look around, Twinket."

The doll and the spriggan girl trotted down the bridge faster than the others and disappeared among a family of ogres. When Aislin reached the shore, she paused to look around, too. A group of satyrs were gamboling in a nearby field of wildflowers. A small herd of deer had stopped at the edge of the field to watch as they kicked up their heels while calling to each other in a sharp, barking kind of language.

Fairy warriors trotted past, intent on protecting the fey. Sprites chased each other through the trees. When one spotted a honeycomb, they all gathered around it, taking turns poking it with a stick and swatting away the bees. Aislin was wondering why the sprites weren't getting stung when a voice called out, "Your Highness, we just wanted to say goodbye before we go."

A group of knapsack-carrying gnomes had stopped at the edge of the trees. The princess counted at least thirty gnomes, from infants to an elder with a white beard so long that it was braided and wrapped around his neck like a scarf. Aislin recognized a slightly younger gnome as Bobble, who had stopped her when she was on her way from Mount Gora to Deephold.

"I didn't expect to see you here," Aislin told him.

"We decided to return to our ancestral home," Bobble replied.

"Will you have to travel far?" asked Aislin.

"A two-day walk, according to Gramps," the gnome replied, nodding toward the gnome with the extra-long beard. "We're going to see if the old stump is still there. Gramps said he hid it well before he left, so we hope nothing has changed. My brother Gambol won't be joining us. He sent word that he's staying at the castle in Eliasind with his wife and children. He loves it there and says he wouldn't dream of leaving. Please say hello to him for me when you see him."

"I will," Aislin replied. "Safe travels!"

As the gnomes disappeared into the forest, tiny fairies swirled around Aislin before flying off. A raccoon shuffled out from among the trees and walked up to Poppy. He chittered at her for a moment, then headed back the way he had come.

"What did he say?" asked Aislin.

"That everyone in the forest is happy that the fairies are back. He said the forest is so much nicer when we're here."

"That's good to know," Aislin said. "I'd hate to think that the animals didn't want us around."

A young male ogre stomped up to Aislin wearing a terrifying expression. Lin and Deela stepped in front of the princess with their hands on their weapons, guarding her until he got close enough that they could see his smile. "Surprise!" Kimble shouted, popping up from behind the ogre's shoulder. Twinket appeared behind his other shoulder, grinning.

"They wanted to see what it was like from up here, so I gave them a ride," the ogre explained.

"This is fun!" Kimble cried. "Can we keep him?"

Aislin laughed and shook her head. "I'm sure this gentle-ogre has plans of his own. He can't spend all his time entertaining you two."

"We didn't hitch a ride just for fun!" said Twinket. "We came to tell you that humans have been spotted in the forest coming this way."

"Then we need to go inside to change our clothes and prepare for their arrival. That means you, too, Twinket and Kimble," Aislin said when the ogre started to turn, still carrying his passengers. "You do have a job to do."

Kimble leaned over to whisper in Twinket's ear. The doll smiled at her and nodded before they both scrambled down the ogre's back.

"Thanks for the ride!" Twinket called as the ogre lumbered away.

"Any time," he told them, waving.

Kimble grabbed Twinket's hand and they ran toward the crystal bridge together.

"I think those two are planning something," Poppy whispered to Aislin.

Aislin sighed. "I'm sure you're right, and it's bound to cause trouble, whatever it is."

Aislin had just put on the primrose-yellow gown that had been draped across her bed when three fairies flew through her window. "Queen Surinen sent us to fix your hair," they said, fluttering around her. "Please stand still. She said that we need to be quick about it. The humans will be here soon and everyone is expecting you in the throne room."

"Can you do my hair, too?" Twinket asked from her seat on the table. She had dressed in a bluebell-colored gown trimmed with tiny silver bells. When she stood up, the bells made a soft, sweet sound.

"We'll see," said one of the fairies.

Aislin stood with her eyes closed as the fairies

darted around her, tugging out her braids, combing out her hair, then putting it up. They poked and prodded, yanked and patted; it all took less than a minute. When they were done, two of them held up her hand mirror while another said, "Open your eyes."

The princess smiled when she saw her reflection. They had arranged her hair in soft curls around her face, using primrose-headed pins to hold it up. The rest of her long, dark hair cascaded down her back with more primroses tucked into the curls.

"Now me!" Twinket cried. "You have time. I can run really fast if I have to."

The fairies laughed, and the sound was even sweeter than Twinket's bells.

"We'll do it!" two fairies exclaimed. Zipping around so fast that they were almost a blur, the fairies rearranged the doll's fine yarn hair on top of her head, adding even more silver bells.

"Hurry!" the fairies told the princess.

Aislin picked up Twinket and ran to the door. Her other ladies were waiting for her in the chamber just outside. They were all wearing dresses that complemented the princess's gown, in shades of cream and blue with mestari emblems on their shoulders.

Aislin thought they all looked lovely. After pausing just long enough to greet them, she led them out the door and down the corridor.

"Use the magic door!" Poppy suggested, and the princess nodded.

The magic door was one of the fairy queen's creations. Located near the royal suites, it took one directly to the throne room on the opposite side of the palace. Only a member of the royal family could open it, though once it was open, anyone could pass through.

The girls waited while Aislin opened the door, revealing a sparkling light just inside. Stepping over the threshold, she found herself facing the raised dais made of moss-covered boulders where the thrones made of arched and curled living branches stood. A chipmunk peeked out at her from among the rocks, while a wren twittered from the back of the king's throne. As the princess approached her family down the aisle through the throng of waiting fey, her ladies came through the door one after the other.

"Good, you're here," said Queen Surinen. "Your parents have been waiting to say goodbye to you before they leave."

"Your mother and I have to take Timzy back to Eliasind," Aislin's father explained. "We've received word that a person everyone refers to only as 'She' has been spreading rumors that King Darinar is abandoning them and that no one will protect them now. Even worse, a small group attacked the Big Foot, Fluffy, who was on her way to our castle. They pelted her with stones and broke one of her fangs, just because she's a friend of our family. Your mother needs to heal her and I need to find the fairies who did it. I also have to spread the word that all the land between the mountains is now Eliasind and that all the fey who live there are under my protection. When you've finished helping your grandmother, come home to us. We'll have much to do."

Aislin was horrified that fey had attacked poor Fluffy. To think that anyone could be so cruel! And the fact that "She" was still spreading rumors about her family made Aislin feel sick to her stomach. Queen Maylin saw the expression on Aislin's face. "Don't worry, my darling," said the queen. "Your father and I will take care of it."

Aislin felt a little better after her mother hugged her, but she needed to tell them what she knew.

"Someone they call 'She' was spreading rumors about me, too. 'She' convinced some of the fey that I'm the reason that everyone has to move, saying that it was because I liked the human world. 'She' also told them that they don't have a choice and have to go, even if they don't want to."

King Carrigan looked grim when he nodded. "We need to ferret out the identity of the person making up these lies." Pulling Aislin into his arms for a hug, he murmured, "Everything will be fine."

"Come home soon," said Timzy who had been playing with a toy fairy warrior. "I want to go exploring, but Papa says I have to wait until you can go with us."

Aislin laughed. "I'll be as quick as I can," she said, and gave her little brother an extra-long hug.

Only moments after her brother and parents left, Peri, tiny once again, darted into the throne room. Flying directly to the king and queen, he hovered between them to deliver his message, then darted out again.

"The humans are almost here," Queen Surinen announced. "Aislin, come stand on the dais with us."

Leaving her mestari behind, Aislin climbed the rocks of the dais, stepping past the ever-flowing waterfall and skirting the blossoming wildflowers. She loved the scents of the forest that permeated the throne room and thought they were finer than any perfume she'd smelled in the human world.

When she reached the rock just below her grandfather's throne, Aislin asked, "How did the humans get here so fast? We've only just arrived."

King Darinar leaned toward her to reply. "I had made this forest impenetrable when we left, so no human has been able to enter it in our absence. After your grandmother and I decided to return, I sent word to the humans and told them where to look for us. They have been waiting just outside the forest. When we returned, they were once again able to enter. Even so, the humans arriving now must have ridden their swiftest horses to get through the forest this quickly."

A bird trilled and the king looked up. "The humans have entered the palace," he announced. "I thought I'd never see another human here again, but no one can plan for everything."

The fey turned toward the closed doors to wait. Most of them hadn't seen a human in hundreds of years, while others had never seen them at all. Some waited with anticipation, some with abject dislike, but all of them were curious to see who would be the first to visit the fairy palace.

As the door opened, Aislin was disappointed when it was just Duke Fadding, the Duke of Scarmander, who entered the throne room. But when she saw the person behind him, she couldn't stop smiling. Tomas, the duke's son, had come.

Chapter 11

ALTHOUGH AISLIN WANTED TO call out to Tomas, she knew better than to try. She watched as he approached the throne with his father. At first her friend seemed enthralled with the fey standing on either side of the aisle, gazing warily at the ogres and orcs and curiously at the fairies, satyrs, gnomes, sprites, and nymphs. When a tiny fairy broke protocol and flew higher to get a better look at the humans, Tomas's gaze followed her to the ceiling, watching as clouds seemed to scud by. His mouth dropped open as he and his father neared the dais, which looked as if it were located in the middle of a forest glade, with a turtle basking on a sun-warmed rock at the edge of the waterfall and hummingbirds flitting between pink and purple flowers at the base of blooming dogwood trees.

Duke Fadding stopped yards from the dais and bowed his head. Tomas walked beside him, but he was staring at the fairy king and queen so intently that he would have kept going if his father hadn't put out his hand. When Tomas realized what he was doing, he stopped abruptly beside his father and bowed his head as well.

"Welcome to Fairengar," King Darinar told them. "I trust all is well between Scarmander and Morain?"

Duke Fadding and Tomas looked up. The duke nodded. "Yes, Your Majesty. The accord you helped us reach has held better than any we would have made on our own."

Aislin glanced at her grandfather. After Poppy had contacted them, he and her father had come to find Aislin and had ended up interceeding in the first battle in what might have been a lengthy war. Because the evil fairy Aghamonda had been involved, King Darinar had felt duty bound to negotiate peace between the two kingdoms. Apparently, the humans appreciated his efforts.

Aislin turned back and saw that Tomas had finally

noticed her. He was looking at her with a big grin on his face, too. It made her realize how much she had missed him, and how glad she was to see him again. Eager to talk to her friend about all that had happened since she last saw him, Aislin paid little attention to the rest of the conversation her grandparents had with Duke Fadding.

They were still talking when Peri returned, tiny once again, and spoke to the fairy king and queen, telling them that other humans had arrived and were on their way to the throne room. Before too long, King Markeen of Halugonia, Queen Solange of Soodfriede, and King Arturo of Tamweld arrived. Aislin knew they had come great distances to pay homage to the fairy king and queen.

Although Aislin thought King Markeen's pointed hat covered with jingling bells was funny, she didn't like the way he glanced at the fairies closest to him with distaste. When a fairy smiled at him, he looked dismayed, as if he didn't know what to do. Queen Solange held herself aloof, trying hard not to look at the fey as she walked between their ranks. She seemed nervous when she approached the dais and found it difficult to meet the eyes of King Darinar and Queen

Surinen. King Arturo was a rounded man with a red face who laughed a lot. Aislin thought he laughed too much, including at things that weren't funny. When he stumbled over his own feet, she thought that he might be nervous, too.

King Markeen had also brought his son with him. The sullen young man looked as if he'd rather be anywhere but there. The doors opened again and King Tyburr of Morain walked in with Prince Rory, Princess Selene and Queen Tatya. Aislin was happy to see Selene, although she would have been delighted if she never saw Rory again. Three of Selene's ladies-in-waiting entered, too, along with three of the queen's. They stopped near the back of the room while the royals approached the dais. Aislin knew precisely when the girls spotted her because their jaws dropped and they looked dazed.

Queen Surinen must have seen it, too. She laughed and turned to Aislin. "Are those the girls you mentioned?"

"They are," the princess replied. "I don't think they could look more surprised." Aislin tried not to laugh at the expressions on their faces, so different from the smug disdain they usually wore.

"Tomas hasn't stopped staring at you," said King Darinar. "Why don't you go talk to him?"

"If you're sure it's all right," Aislin said.

When he nodded, she fairly flew down the stones to work her way between the fey to Tomas's side. Curious, the fey she passed turned to watch her.

"Welcome to Fairengar," she said as she joined her friend.

The fey near Tomas leaned closer as if to listen in.

"Thanks," Tomas said, his face lighting up. "I hoped you'd be here. It was the reason I asked Father to bring me."

"I'm here to help the fey settle in, then I'm going back to Eliasind."

"I hope it takes a long time for them to settle in," Tomas said with a grin.

Aislin laughed. Her heart felt lighter now that Tomas was here. Even when they were stuck in Morain, he'd had a knack for making her feel better.

"King Ozwalt didn't come?" Aislin asked him, looking around.

Tomas shook his head. "His health is failing and he doesn't go far from his bed anymore. Father has been taking on more and more responsibilities lately.

153

"So this is Fairengar," he said, looking around, his eyes wide in awe. "I thought that was the kingdom in the land between the mountains."

"The royal palace of the fairies and its surrounding land is called Fairengar, no matter where it is," Aislin explained. "This area actually used to be part of Fairengar once before, and now it is again."

Another voice broke into their conversation. "Aislin, I'm so happy to see you!" Princess Selene cried as she slipped between the fey.

The last time they'd seen each other was when the two princesses had been traveling together. Soldiers had mistaken Aislin for Selene and taken her away. So much had happened since!

"I was so worried about you," said Selene. "I'm sorry to have put you in danger. I should have been the one to go with them."

"It's all right," Aislin told her. "It wasn't your fault that they took me instead. It turned out that they were Tomas's men and everything worked out in the end."

"I'm so relieved to hear you say that," Selene cried. "I was afraid that they'd been horrible to you and that it was all my fault. I couldn't bear to think that my first real friend might have suffered because of me."

The three girls who trailed behind Selene had been nasty to Aislin when she'd stayed in the castle in Morain. Seeing Aislin now, they clustered around the half-fairy princess and gave her ingratiating smiles.

"It's so good to see you again!" Laneece gushed.

"We've all missed you!" cried Joselle.

"You look wonderful!" Merrilee exclaimed. "That color is so slimming on you."

"Merrilee!" Joselle said, scowling at her friend as she nudged her.

The three girls turned and smiled coyly as Rory walked up. "There's my betrothed!" the prince said, shouldering a nymph out of his way. Aislin shuddered. She knew that King Tyburr had wanted to set her up with his son, but as far as she knew, Rory disliked her as much as she disliked him.

If this hadn't been a formal event, Aislin would have told Rory exactly what she thought of him. Instead, she knew she had to be polite, or as close to it as she could come with Rory around. But it didn't mean that she had to let him touch her, as he clearly planned to do. When he continued to approach, and leaned in—as if he was going to kiss her!—Aislin held up her hand to fend him off.

"I'm not your anything," she replied. "And don't come any closer."

Rory's expression flicked sour for a second, but then turned back into a smile. "But I thought we had an understanding," Rory said, opening his eyes wide as if that would make him look innocent.

"You're not fooling anyone, Rory, so cut it out," Tomas told him. "Neither Aislin nor I have forgotten how you treated us in Morain. You lost your chance to be our friend back then."

"People can change," Rory said, looking belligerent.

"You haven't changed one bit," Selene told him.

The fey around them started to turn toward the exit. Aislin realized that her grandparents were no longer on the dais; the royal audience was over.

"I need to go freshen up," Selene said, glancing down at her rumpled dress. "Two days in a carriage didn't do me any favors."

"We'll see you at the ball tonight," Rory told Aislin.

Aislin nodded and tried not to show her surprise. When she thought about it, she decided that she should have expected that her grandparents had planned a ball for that evening; it would explain why she needed that beautiful gown. The ball itself would be so much fun. Too bad Rory was going to be there.

Although Aislin had owned many beautiful gowns, the moonbeam dress Sage and Parsley had created was something special. Only fairies could weave moonbeams, and only the very best fairy seamstresses could gather them from a full moon and create a fabric that shimmered with its own special light. Sage and Parsley were in fact the very best fairy seamstresses who had ever lived. And to make the gown even more dazzling, they had added thousands of diamonds, letting it sparkle and shine.

The two fairies had come to help Aislin put on the gown in case it needed any last-minute adjustments. When she slipped it over her head and smoothed it over her hips, she already felt beautiful, but when Sage produced a mirror in front of her and flicked her fingers to dim the fairy lights in the room, the princess gasped. While the gown would have been lovely in the daylight, it was beyond extraordinary now that the sun had set. This dress had been crafted especially for her and fit her perfectly. It had already been glowing when she put it on, but her pedrasi side took strength from the diamonds themselves, and sent it back into the moonbeams, making the light even stronger. Aislin looked like a celestial being come down to earth.

The gown was more than just beautiful. Aislin had never worn a gown embellished with any kind of stones before. As she stood there gazing at her reflection, she could feel power from the diamonds leaching into her, making her blood thrum as it coursed through her veins. The power from each kind of stone was different. A diamond's was pure and clean. It was one of the most invigorating stones she'd ever felt.

"I feel wonderful!" she told the fairy seamstresses. "Could you add diamonds to all my clothes?"

"That might be a little extreme," said Sage. "You don't need to wear gowns this beautiful all the time."

Aislin brushed the diamonds on the gown's bodice with her fingertip. It was enough to give her another surge of power. "I don't want them for the way they look. I want them for the power they give me. They wouldn't even have to be anywhere you can see them."

"Ah, this would be for your pedrasi side," Sage said. "I understand. I'll see what I can do."

Aislin was still admiring the dress when the same fairies who had fixed her hair before flew through the window to create an even lovelier hairstyle, only this time they tucked diamonds into her curls instead of flowers. When they had finished, the princess cast one more glance at her reflection and turned toward the door. If her grandmother wanted her to impress the humans, this dress was perfect.

Aislin stepped into the corridor and found all her ladies waiting for her. They were wearing their very best gowns and the bodice of each gown bore the mestari emblem in silver, which seemed to glow of its own accord. Deela's and Lin's gowns had lots of pleats and folds, some of which concealed the weapons that they insisted they needed. Poppy's dress was made of newly opened buds and smelled wonderful, while Twinket and Kimble were dressed in spider-silk gowns with matching leggings, just as they'd requested. The mestari all looked lovely, though none could compare to Aislin and her moonbeam gown.

"Wow!" Deela exclaimed. "I've never seen that many diamonds in my life!"

"I've never seen such a beautiful gown!" said Lin.

"You don't look real!" Poppy said in a half whisper.

"Will those stones come off if I touch you?" Twinket asked. "I don't want to knock any off if you pick me up."

"No, they won't come off," Sage assured her. "Not even if someone tried."

"I don't know what the big fuss is about," said Kimble. "It's just a dress. Let's go get this thing over with. I hate wearing dresses and this one itches."

Aislin stepped over the threshold of the door leading into the great hall, but the room wasn't at all what she'd expected. Instead of the vast room where everyone ate supper, it felt as if she was outside in the forest. Twinkling stars surrounded the moon shining overhead. A gentle breeze caressed her cheek, smelling of loam and leaves, pine needles and wildflowers. Waist-high red mushrooms with white polka dots surrounded the perimeter of the moss-covered dance floor, making it look like a fairy circle. Closing her eyes, she sensed rock still cooling from the day's heat. She heard an owl hoot and mice scurry into the safety of holes in the ground.

"Her Royal Highness, Princess Aislin of Eliasind,

Fairengar, and Deephold," announced the herald in ringing tones.

There was a gasp as the fey spotted Aislin in her diamond and moonbeam gown. Fairies descended on her before she could take another step. The colors of the ladies' gowns and the gentlemen's tunics reflected off her diamonds, dazzling in the light of the corridor.

"You look so beautiful!" some cried.

"You look amazing!" cried others.

Aislin was pleased to see that her mestari were also receiving admiring glances. And then the music started, and the fey headed off to find partners for the first dance.

When the herald announced the next arrival, the princess walked farther into the room.

"Fairies sure can decorate!" exclaimed Kimble as she followed the princess.

Aislin didn't have time to answer as Selene and her ladies-in-waiting descended on her. Merrilee, Joselle, and Laneece curtseyed so deeply that they looked as if they were about to sit down.

"I love your gown!" Selene cried. "What is it made of?"

"Moonbeams and diamonds," said Aislin.

"Real moonbeams?" Merrilee asked.

Laneece gasped. "Those can't all be real diamonds! It's just not possible."

Tomas had just walked up behind Selene's ladies-in-waiting. As he moved to stand beside Aislin, he gave the human girl a withering look. "You're talking to a fairy princess. Anything is possible for Princess Aislin. Show some respect, Laneece."

"We never guessed that you were a fairy princess," cried Merrilee. "I mean, you look beautiful now, but you looked so dowdy and uninteresting back in Morain. None of us had any idea that you were anything special."

Aislin turned slowly to look at the girl, but couldn't decide if she was intentionally rude or did it without thinking. Either way, Aislin didn't want to have anything to do with her. The look the princess gave Merrilee would have chilled her to the bone, if only she'd been looking at Aislin's face and not her gown.

"Walk away now, before I turn you into a toad," Poppy told Merrilee. "And don't say another word to Aislin."

Merrilee looked outraged. She asked Aislin, "Are you going to let her talk to me like that?"

Aislin shrugged. "I don't know why not. These are my mestari, so they outrank you in every way possible. They may talk to you however they please. Poppy has every right to turn you into a toad."

"What's a mestari?" asked Laneece.

"It's like a super special lady-in-waiting plus the queen's champion and guard," Kimble said, holding her head high. "I'm one, too."

"I'm an honorable one," Twinket boasted.

"Is that a talking doll?" Merrilee said, her eyes huge. "How very odd!"

Aislin looked at Poppy and said, "Just make sure you turn her back before the night is out."

"No problem," Poppy replied. "Although I can't promise that there won't be any aftereffects." She pointed at Merrilee, her finger surrounded by purple sparkles. There was a puff of purple dust and a toad squatted where the lady-in-waiting had been standing.

Selene's other two ladies-in-waiting gasped and turned pale, but Selene just said, "It's about time someone stood up to her. I told Merrilee that she had to learn to be nicer to people."

"We don't want her to get stepped on, now do we?" Deela said. She bent down and scooped up the toad, then carried it toward one of the mushrooms that edged the dance floor.

"Is that thing an orc?" Joselle croaked. "I've never seen one up close before. And it's wearing a very pretty gown. Why would you dress up a monster like that? Is it one of your mess...whatevers, too?"

"Selene, it seems your ladies never change," said Aislin. "Do you mind if Poppy takes care of her, as well?"

"Please do," Selene said. "They all need to learn to be nicer."

"No!" cried Joselle. "I didn't mean...I was just..."

Once again purple sparkles surrounded Poppy's finger and a lady-in-waiting transformed into a toad. Deela came back from moving the first toad in time to see it happen. "Not another one!" she said. "What did this one say?"

Lin leaned toward her friend and whispered into her ear. The orc's face got darker and she glared at the toad. "I'm not moving this one," she said. "It can take its chances with the dancers."

Music began to play and Aislin glanced toward

164

the side of the room where fairies, pedrasi, satyrs, and a gnome played drums, pipes, and bandolinos. It took two fairies to play a long stringed instrument that she'd never seen before.

Fey and humans drifted into the middle of the dance floor as the musicians began the music for another dance. Aislin was looking around when she felt a tug on the back of her gown and heard a crackling sound, and then Laneece cried out.

"That hurt!" Laneece exclaimed, looking indignant. "Your dress shocked me!"

"That's a great anti-theft system you've got there, Princess!" exclaimed Kimble. "I saw the whole thing. Lady Sticky-Fingers tried to take one of your diamonds, but it sparked and turned her fingers red. Just look at them!"

They all glanced at Laneece's hand. The fingers on her right hand were now bright red, as if they had been dipped in paint. She examined them, turning her hand front to back. Aislin thought the girl looked more puzzled than hurt.

"This color will come off, won't it?" she asked Poppy.

"Don't look at me," the fairy replied. "That wasn't

my spell. But I'd guess that it's permanent. You were a thief who was caught red-handed and now the whole world will know it."

"I just wanted to see if it was real!" Laneece wailed. "I wasn't going to keep it."

"Yeah, right," said Deela.

Clutching her hand to her chest, Laneece ran back into the corridor.

"Your ladies need to learn that you shouldn't insult or try to steal from the fey. Every unkind thing they do has consequences among our people," Poppy told Selene. Tomas grinned as he glanced at the toad hopping toward Selene's feet. When he looked back up, his face was serious again. "Pardon me," he said to Aislin, "but I notice that you have yet to dance. Would you do me the honor?" He held out his hand, palm up.

"I'd love to," Aislin said, placing her hand on his.

They waited by the edge of the dance floor until the next dance was about to begin. Aislin was familiar with the dance, and Tomas was not, but he managed to catch on quickly. They twirled around the fairy circle to the music until they were both out of breath. The next song was slower and they were actually able to talk.

"Did I tell you that you look amazing?" Tomas asked her. "You have to be the most beautiful girl I've ever seen. You literally took my breath away when I saw you come in."

"Thank you," she said, smiling up at him. Aislin knew that a fairy had given Tomas the gift of truth at his christening, which meant that he always told the truth no matter what. It was nice to know that he really did mean what he said.

"So, you have mestari attending you?" said Tomas. "You never mentioned them before."

"I didn't have them before," Aislin said, glancing between the dancers as she looked for her ladies. Poppy was dancing with a fairy knight with dark green hair while Deela was twirling around in the arms of a satyr. Twinket and Kimble were both dancing with sprites and seemed to be having a wonderful time. She didn't see Lin dancing, but she finally spotted her friend on the side talking to a pedrasi warrior. Aislin was happy to see that her mestari were enjoying themselves and that the fey were treating them with the respect that they deserved.

Suddenly the music demanded that Tomas twirl her. When he was holding her again he said, "This place is unbelievable. I know we're still in the palace, but it really feels as if we're outside. I know that fairies can make glamours that look like the real thing. I just never imagined that they could be this good."

"My grandparents are very powerful fairies," said Aislin. "They can do some amazing things."

"I didn't see your father in the throne room today. Is he here now?" Tomas asked.

Aislin shook her head. "My parents had to return to Eliasind. Not all fey are happy about the move and some are causing trouble because of it."

"I'm sorry to hear that," Tomas said. "I like your father, and I was looking forward to meeting your mother."

Aislin smiled. "You'd like my mother. She's a wonderful person and—"

"May I cut in?" asked a pedrasi warrior named Kivi as the dance ended. "I understand that's allowed among humans and I thought I'd give it a try."

"Yes, it is a custom in some places," said Tomas. "But not one I like," he added under his breath.

He looked disappointed as he stepped away from Aislin, but then the music started up again and Kivi whirled her away across the fairy circle and she lost sight of Tomas. "You look amazing," Kivi said in a loud voice. "We met in Deephold a few times, but you might not remember me. I was training to be a guard and..."

Aislin tried to listen while the pedrasi talked about himself, but she couldn't stop looking for Tomas. She danced the next dance with Captain Larch, the captain of the fairy guard. A satyr asked her to dance after that, and then a male fairy courtier whom she had seen around but never met. After that, Sycamore, Captain Larch's second-in-command, asked her for a dance, as well.

The dance had just ended when King Darinar approached and held out his hand. Aislin smiled up at her grandfather, relieved that she didn't have to make small talk with someone she didn't know very well.

"Are you enjoying yourself?" asked her grandfather.

"Very much," said Aislin. "This is a lovely ball and your musicians are outdoing themselves. And the glamour you created for the ballroom is amazing."

King Darinar laughed. "That was all your grandmother's doing. I saw you dancing with Tomas and now he can't keep his eyes off you."

Aislin felt herself blush, but all she said was, "We're just friends."

"And what about King Tyburr's son? He's been watching you all evening as well."

"That's Rory and he is *not* a friend," said Aislin.

"Ah, yes, I remember now. He's the one who was so rude to you. Would you like me to turn him into something small and quiet for the rest of the evening? I haven't turned anyone into a mouse in years."

Aislin laughed and shook her head. "That won't be necessary, but thank you for the offer."

The dance ended a few minutes later and a fairy courtier named Rye came to ask for the next one. He was sweeping her around the circle when she spotted Tomas dancing with Selene. When Rye twirled her around, Tomas and Selene disappeared among the other dancers. As Aislin was looking for them a few minutes later, she saw Rory watching her from the side. Feeling his eyes on her was enough to make her uncomfortable. She really didn't want to dance with him, but when he approached during the next not-so-fast song and asked to cut in, she couldn't be rude and refuse.

Although Aislin didn't want Rory to touch her, she also didn't want to make a scene, so she took his hand when he offered it and let him twirl her through the dancers. To her surprise, Rory took her past the mushrooms so that they were outside the ring.

"What are you doing?" she asked, pulling away from him.

"I just wanted to talk," he replied. "I couldn't think of any other way to get you alone."

Aislin sighed. "We don't have anything to talk about, Rory. I don't like you and I know you don't like me, despite what you said earlier."

"That's not true!" Rory exclaimed. "I do like you and I think we could have a real future together. I was a fool to treat you the way I did in Morain and I'd like to make it up to you."

Aislin didn't believe him, no matter how sincere he was trying to look. She let him ramble on while she glanced back at the dancers inside the fairy ring. It struck her as odd that none of the flower fairies had gotten small so they could dance in the air the way they usually did. Everything seemed incredibly real, too. The glamour was so perfect that she could have sworn she heard animals rustling in the forest around them, even though she knew she was standing in the great hall and—

"If you won't listen to me, maybe this will get

your attention," Rory said, pulling her into his arms for a kiss.

It was the first time a boy had ever really tried to kiss her and she wasn't at all happy about it. She'd thought her first kiss would be something special, not forced on her by someone she didn't even like. It was unpleasant, too, kind of squishy and greasy, like he'd just eaten something fried and forgotten to wipe his mouth afterward. Putting her hands on his shoulders, she pushed him so that he fell back and sat down heavily.

"Don't ever touch me again!" she told him.

"I just wanted to show you what you'd be missing if you keep turning me down," Rory said, sounding sullen.

Something above them made a sound, drawing her gaze. A giant rabbit loomed over them, twitching its nose and whiskers. Aislin let out a small shriek; it was enough to make Rory tilt his head back to look up. "What is that?" he whispered to Aislin.

"A rabbit," she told him.

Looking around, she noted how impossibly tall the trees looked, how cushy the moss felt underfoot, and that a fallen leaf seemed unusually huge. She knew her grandmother's glamours were exceptional, but she doubted that even the fairy queen could create one that was this detailed and complete. Besides, if her intent was to make a glamour of a fairy ring, why go so far as to include the forest around it? That didn't make any sense, unless it wasn't a glamour at all.

Suddenly, Aislin realized that her grandmother must have done something even more impressive than create a realistic glamour. She had turned the door to the great hall into a magic portal that took anyone who stepped through to a real fairy ring. Not only did the portal transport them, it also shrank them down to the size of a tiny fairy. No wonder the fairies didn't try to get smaller! They were already tiny, although this time they didn't have their wings.

"Wow!" Aislin exclaimed. "This is amazing."

"What?" asked Rory. "None of this is real."

The rabbit crouched lower to sniff them. Its breath stirred Aislin's dress and ruffled Rory's hair so that it fell into his eyes.

"Actually, I think it is," Aislin told him. "This isn't a glamour."

"You mean that's a giant rabbit?" Rory squeaked.

"No," said Aislin. "I think it's probably the normal size for a rabbit. It's just that we're tiny."

"Don't be ridiculous," Rory snapped. "I'm the same size I've always been."

Aislin glanced from Rory to the rabbit, to the mushrooms to the trees. "So, you're the same and everything else became huge?"

Rory shrank back as the rabbit snuffled his hair again. "I might be wrong," the prince said even as he inched toward the mushroom ring. "Tell me, are we stuck like this for good? Because I never gave my permission for any of this. My father is going to be furious when he finds out."

"Your father is at the ball, so he's small now, too. And this isn't permanent," Aislin assured him. "Once you go back through that door, I'm sure you'll be your old self again."

"Good," Rory said. "We'll talk again later."

Aislin watched him dart back between the mushrooms and head straight for the door. She was sure that most people would enjoy the chance to be tiny for a while, but apparently Rory wasn't one of them. Regardless of the reason for his sudden departure, she was glad that he was gone.

Chapter 12

AFTER A LATE NIGHT at the ball, Aislin had looked forward to sleeping in. She'd told her ladies about her plans, so she wasn't expecting to have Poppy knock and walk into her bedchamber early the next morning.

"I hate to disturb you," the fairy said, "but the guards want to know what they should do with Twinket and Kimble."

Aislin opened her eyes to peer at her friend. "What do you mean?" she asked.

"The captain of the guards told me that Twinket and Kimble were caught painting pictures of fairies in the great hall. On the walls. Life-sized. I've seen them. The pictures are actually very well done; you can tell exactly who they're supposed to be. The fairies they painted are furious."

"Where are Twinket and Kimble now?" Aislin asked, suddenly awake.

"They're under guard in the great hall," said Poppy. "The captain won't release them until he talks to you."

"Then I guess I'm getting up," Aislin said, and slid out of bed.

She was about to throw on an old dress until she remembered that there were visiting humans in the palace. Looking anything but her best wasn't a good idea now. Although it took her longer than she would have liked, she washed her face and brushed her hair before putting on a jade green dress with vines embroidered on the sleeves that Sage and Parsley had left for her. Except for the two culprits, all her mestari were waiting in her sitting room. They followed her as she hurried down the corridor.

"I had a feeling Twinket and Kimble were planning some sort of mischief," Aislin told Poppy. "All that whispering and giggling yesterday had to mean something. I ignored it though, because I was glad they'd become friends."

"I've never seen Twinket this happy before," Poppy replied.

"I know, but she's never done anything like this before either. I'm starting to think that Kimble may not be a good influence on her."

Aislin heard voices as she approached the great hall; the fairies who were gathered outside the door scattered as soon as they caught sight of the princess and her mestari. She found Twinket and Kimble seated at the side of the hall with three fairy guards watching over them. They were all laughing when she walked up and grew quiet when they saw her. Two of the guards stepped away from the wall, revealing the paintings.

Aislin knew she should be angry, but she couldn't keep from laughing when she saw what Twinket and Kimble had done. The paintings were more caricatures of the fairies than realistic likenesses, emphasizing their more obvious traits. The fairy who smiled in response to everything wore an enormous grin. The tallest fairy had bean tendrils wrapped around her as if she were an actual beanpole. The quietest fairy had her finger in front of her lips, shushing everyone. The most boisterous fairy had her head thrown back and was laughing in a way that made anyone who saw it want to laugh, too.

"I'm sorry for disturbing you, Your Highness,"

said Captain Larch, "but I wanted you to see this. The paintings were already here when my men came through before dawn and we've had complaints all morning. Your ladies shouldn't have painted these and they need to be punished. They are your ladies, however, and you should be the one to decide how to handle this."

"Are they in trouble because they painted these particular pictures, which I think are actually very nice," Aislin said, "or was it because of where they painted the pictures?"

The captain glanced at the pictures again. He chuckled when his eyes fell on the laughing fairy. His eyes were still shining when he turned back to Aislin. "It's the location, Your Highness. This isn't an art gallery."

"I see," said Aislin. "Thank you, Captain. I'll take care of it. If I might have a moment to speak to my mestari alone?"

"Of course," he said. Gesturing to his guards, they all left the hall.

"Whatever were you thinking?" Aislin asked Twinket and Kimble.

"That it would be fun," Twinket told her and grinned at Kimble. "And it was!"

Aislin sighed. "You should never paint pictures where it isn't allowed. The great hall is definitely one of those places."

"How were we supposed to know that?" asked Kimble. "I painted the walls in the cave where I lived with my parents and everybody liked it."

"That's different," said Aislin. "This palace belongs to the fairy king and queen and you can paint only if you get permission first. Your paintings are very good, but you didn't ask first, so you have to clean them off the walls."

"But we put a lot of work into them!" wailed Twinket.

"And we stayed up all night to do them," Kimble added.

"Even so, you should have asked before you started painting," Aislin replied. "Poppy, can you give them soap and scrub brushes that will take this paint off and leave the walls as good as new?"

With a flick of her fingers, Poppy made everything they needed appear on the floor in front of them.

"If she can do that, why can't Poppy just wiggle her fingers and clean the walls?" asked Kimble.

"Because Poppy didn't paint the walls and it's not up to her to clean them," Aislin told her.

"Poppy, Lin, and I will stay to make sure Twinket and Kimble don't miss anything," said Deela.

"Good," Aislin replied. "I have something to take care of now. Bring them to my chambers when they're finished."

Twinket and Kimble were already scrubbing the wall when Aislin hurried back to her rooms. She knew what she wanted to find; she just didn't know where to start looking. Her fairy grandparents were aware that she loved to read, so they'd given her lots of books that they thought she might enjoy. Although the books were neatly stored in niches in her walls, they weren't in any order, so it took her a while to find the ones she wanted.

Aislin's arms were loaded down with books when she returned to her sitting room. She stacked the books on the table, then took out a leaf and a writing stick. She was still working on her notes when her ladies knocked and walked in.

"Are you finished?" she asked Twinket and Kimble.

"Yeah, although it was a real shame," Kimble told her. "That was some of my best work!"

"It was very good," said Aislin. "Which is why I

want you to do some painting for me. These are my rooms, and my grandparents told me long ago that I can decorate them however I please. I'd love for you to paint murals on the walls. I have some books that might give you ideas of the scenes I'd like you to include." She patted the stack of books on her table. Small leaves stuck out of the books to mark the places she wanted them to see. "I made notes of everything I want. It's all right here."

"Do you want us to start now?" asked Twinket.

"Not this minute," Aislin said. "I thought we could all go outside for some fresh air and see how the fey are settling down. Maybe we'll get more ideas for the murals, too."

Her mestari were just as eager as she was to see how magic was changing the world around them. This time when they crossed the crystal bridge to the shore, they stayed by the lake instead of going into the forest. Kimble was excited about the murals and kept pointing out trees and water views that she'd like to include in her paintings. Twinket spotted a jack-in-the-pulpit that she wanted to paint.

The little doll was bending down to examine the plant when the rest of the mestari noticed that Selene and her ladies were only a short distance away. "Look at that!" Poppy exclaimed, pointing at Merrilee and Joselle who were both making jerky, hopping movements as they followed the human princess. "I told you that there might be side effects!"

"Once a toad, aways a toad," said Deela.

Kimble started grinning when she saw Laneece. "She's wearing gloves to cover her red fingers. I bet she wears them all the time now. Maybe that will teach her not to try to steal from the fey!"

"We'll have to tell Sage and Parsley just how well their anti-theft spell worked!" said Lin.

Aislin laughed. "I'm sure this is one trip that none of them will ever forget."

"Come on, Twinket," Kimble told her friend. "You've looked at that jack-in-the-pulpit long enough. We have places to go and more plants to see." Aislin and her mestari had walked partway around the palace when they suddenly heard the shrill shrieking of tiny fairies in distress coming from the forest. "Stay here, Your Highness," Deela said, setting her hand on her sword. "I'll go see what's happening. Lin, protect the princess."

The pedrasi girl nodded and took her war hammer from her belt. As the orc ran off, Lin scanned the forest on one side and the water on the other, looking for anything unusual.

"I found the problem!" Deela called from among the trees. "It's safe to come here now."

Aislin and the other ladies ran into the forest to join her. They found the orc bent over three tiny fairies on a moss-covered boulder. Buttercup was sitting down, Dandelion was kneeling, and Cornflower was crouched with one hand on the moss. All three of them were holding fragrant honeysuckle blossoms in their free hands, and their eyes were red from crying.

"Please help us," cried the fairy named Buttercup. "We're stuck and our magic isn't working."

"The moss is covered with sticky pine sap, even though there aren't any pine trees in this part of the forest," Deela explained. "We'll have to pry the fairies off."

Aislin was confused. There didn't seem to be anything special about the boulder—certainly nothing that would attract a flower fairy.

"Why did you land here?" Aislin asked them.

"We followed the scent of these luscious honeysuckle blossoms," said Cornflower. "They were lying right here on this rock."

"There aren't any honeysuckle vines near here

183

though," Aislin said as she looked around. "Someone must have done this purposefully to trap fairies."

"What a horrid thing to do!" cried Poppy.

"Can't you turn big and get free yourself?" Kimble asked the fairies.

Buttercup shook her head as tears trickled down her cheeks. "We tried, but our magic doesn't work at all now."

Poppy held out her hand. The air around it began to sparkle, but when she sent her magic to the tiny fairies, the sparkles died away as soon as they got close to the moss. She pursed her lips and concentrated. When nothing happened, she said, "We can't use my magic to help them either."

"We'll have to find some way to free them before whoever did this comes back," Aislin told her mestari.

"If you take a piece of bark, you can work it under the fairies into the moss and scrape them off the rock," said Lin. "We use pieces of slate to scrape algae off the rocks back home."

"Good idea," said Aislin. "Then we can take them back to the palace and Queen Surinen can find out why the fairies' magic doesn't work. Just be careful, we don't want to hurt them."

They had all started looking for pieces of bark big enough to use when they heard the high, shrill scream of more tiny fairies. "I'll go this time," Lin announced, and took off deeper into the forest. Aislin watched her remaining friends for a moment, glad that she'd chosen ladies who really cared about others. She doubted that any of Selene's ladies-in-waiting would have even tried to help the fairies.

They were still trying to free the original fairies when Lin came rushing back. "I found more fairies just like these," the pedrasi girl told them. "Twinket, Kimble, come with me."

The three of them ran off, leaving Deela and Poppy with Aislin. When they heard more screaming start in another direction, Poppy said, "I'll go," and hurried away, taking a piece of bark with her.

Only Deela and Aislin were left to take care of the first fairies they'd found. They were scraping away at the moss when even more fairies started screaming down by the lake. Deela looked up, then back at the princess. "I don't want to leave you alone," she said. "Maybe you should come with me."

"Don't abandon us!" Cornflower shouted at Aislin, and all three tiny fairies burst into tears again.

"Go!" Aislin told Deela. "I'll be fine here. I almost have Dandelion free."

"If you're sure..." said the orc girl.

Aislin nodded. "We can't leave the fairies alone and frightened."

"Call me if you need me and I'll come running," Deela told her.

"I will," Aislin said, and went back to work, determined to free the fairies by herself.

Aislin was trying so hard to free the fairies without hurting them that she didn't hear the person who crept up behind her. And then he was opening a small green vial under her nose, letting gray mist curl out. The princess realized what was happening just before she and the three tiny fairies collapsed, senseless.

Aislin dreamed that she was floating through the forest, but the ride was bumpy and not very comfortable. Her arm was warm, which she thought was odd. She came to her senses enough to figure out that the fairy seamstresses had done what she'd asked and already started sewing the stones into her dresses. They had put a diamond in the sleeve, and it had worked just as she'd hoped—she was already drawing power from it.

Aislin kept her eyes closed even as she felt the blackness that had taken over her mind fade away and her body grow stronger. She felt the same way she had upon waking from the sleeping mist that the fairy Aghamonda had used on her and knew that it would take a few minutes before she felt normal again.

Someone was carrying her through the forest, pausing now and then as if to listen. She could hear her abductor's heart pounding in his chest right behind her ear. His breath rasped as he ran. When he stopped again, she heard the sounds of a restless horse snapping a twig with its hooves and snorting as her abductor approached it.

Not knowing who was carrying her off, Aislin was reluctant to open her eyes. Her abductor had to be strong, but then a lot of fey were much stronger than they looked. She didn't think it was the mysterious female who was spreading rumors about her, but what if it was? Who else could be doing this and why? If her abductor wanted to hurt her, wouldn't it have happened already?

Aislin knew too much about the many kinds of

fey to be naive about what they were capable of doing. Certain fey were even more bloodthirsty than the wildest of beasts. If the person who was spreading rumors had turned even one of them against Aislin, the princess would have a real fight on her hands.

Her abductor was laying her across the horse's back when Aislin finally slitted her eyes open. It was Rory, which was a relief in a way. He was an ordinary human and not one of the nastier kinds of fey. And the fact that it was Rory didn't surprise her at all once she thought about it—not after the way he had acted the night before.

Aislin didn't want to let him know that she was awake until she was certain that no one else was working with him, so she let her head flop against his shoulder and looked around with her eyes barely open. Finally, seeing that he was alone, she twisted in his arms and elbowed him in the nose.

"Ow!" Rory shouted and dropped her.

Aislin was only partly on the horse's back, so it was easy to slide to the ground. Turning around, she stomped on Rory's instep.

"Ow!" he shouted again and lurched backward, only to trip over a stump and fall to the ground. Blood flowed between the fingers he held to his nose and he lay on the ground, looking up at her accusingly.

"You were *kidnapping* me?" she said, glaring at him.

"You didn't leave me any choice," said Rory. "My father will be so happy if I marry you, he won't even think about having another son. He's very impressed with you now that he knows who you are and what you're capable of doing."

Aislin was so mad she was shaking. "I don't care what you or your father thinks. I'm never going to marry you."

"Princess Aislin!" Deela shouted from back the way they'd come.

"Now see what you've done," griped Rory. "We could have gotten away if you hadn't punched me. I thought you were still asleep."

Aislin shook her head. "I didn't punch you; I used my elbow."

She called out to Deela. "I'm over here!"

Rory started to get up, but Aislin set her foot on his chest and pushed him down. When he tried to shove her off, she pressed until he grunted and gave in. "I'm not going to hurt you. Just stay put!" she told him.

She was still standing like that when Poppy flew

up, tiny and shaken. The fairy landed beside her and became big again only to glance from the princess to Rory. "I should have known Rory was behind this. Are you all right?"

"I'm fine," said Aislin. "I think this whole thing wasn't about the fairies. It was just Rory's way of getting me alone so he could kidnap me."

"I was only—" Rory began.

"Don't say another word," Aislin told him. "You'll get your chance to explain yourself to my grandparents."

Rory's face turned pale under the blood still seeping from his nose.

Deela and Lin ran up, carrying the two little mestari. The moment Lin stopped, Twinket jumped out of her arms and darted over to hug Aislin's leg.

"I knew I shouldn't have left you alone!" Deela exclaimed.

"It's not your fault," said Aislin. "I told you to go. We're taking Prince Rory back to the palace. He's going to talk to King Darinar and Queen Surinen, whether he wants to or not."

Chapter 13

IT WASN'T LONG BEFORE the fairies still sticky with pinesap were on their way to the palace to tell everyone what had happened. Long before Aislin and her ladies crossed the crystal bridge, word about Rory's treachery had spread. Captain Larch met them at the palace gates and had his fairies take Rory into custody. When Aislin and her mestari reached the throne room, King Darinar and Queen Surinen were already seated on their thrones, waiting for them. King Tyburr was there as well, looking furious. Aislin wasn't sure if he was angry because of what his son had done, or because Rory was being escorted into the room under guard.

When Aislin and her mestari went to stand to the left of the aisle leading to the throne, Captain Larch's fairies took Rory to the right. The prince just stood there, looking sullen and refusing to meet his father's eyes or even look in the direction of Aislin's grandparents.

"I understand that Prince Rory laid traps for my fairies," Queen Surinen said to Aislin.

"He did, and then when my mestari were distracted helping the fairies, he tried to kidnap me," Aislin told her.

"Pardon me, Your Majesty, but we don't know for certain that Prince Rory was involved in any of this," said his father.

"Would his confession be enough to convince you?" the fairy queen asked King Tyburr.

"It would," said the king, and turned to his son. "Did you make traps for the fairies?"

"Of course not! I would never do anything like that," said Rory. "I had gone for a walk in the woods when the fairies tied me up and brought me here for no reason at all."

"I'm not convinced that he's telling the truth," King Darinar said.

"My son would never lie!" protested King Tyburr.

"In that case, a truth spell shouldn't make any difference," said the fairy queen. "Prince Rory, I command you to tell the truth for the rest of your life and to answer every question we ask you." Silver sparkles shot from her pointed finger and swirled around Rory. He batted at the sparkles even as they landed on his head.

"I don't want to," Rory cried.

"I'm sure *that's* the truth," Twinket whispered to Aislin.

"Now he'll know what it was like for Tomas," Aislin murmured back.

"What do you mean?" asked Twinket.

Aislin realized that she had never told her friends about the christening gift a fairy had given to Tomas when he was an infant.

"I'll tell you about it later," Aislin told the doll.

"Prince Rory of Morain, did you lay traps for my fairies and try to kidnap my granddaughter, Princess Aislin?" said the fairy queen.

The prince clapped his hands over his mouth, but the words came out anyway. "I laid the traps because I had to make Aislin's mestari leave her by herself. Fairies in distress were the only thing I could think of to draw her ladies away. When she was alone, it was easy to knock her out with the sleeping mist."

"It felt like the same mist that Aghamonda had used on Poppy and Tomas and me in the castle in Scarmander," Aislin told them.

"No wonder you conked out!" exclaimed Poppy. "That stuff was awful."

Thunder rumbled over the palace when King Darinar growled, "Prince Rory, why did you want to kidnap Aislin?"

Rory struggled to remain silent, but the fairy queen's magic was too strong for him to resist. "I said it was because my father wanted me to marry the princess—"

"I never told you to do any of this!" his father roared.

"—but it was really because *She* told me to bring Aislin to her!" Rory finally blurted out.

"So 'She' was involved!" said Aislin.

"Who is 'She'?" demanded the queen. "Where were you supposed to take Aislin?"

Rory's face contorted as he tried not to talk, but the queen's spell was too compelling. "She's a very powerful sorceress named Gorinda. She said that she'd tell me where to go once I'd brought Aislin to Morain." Tears trickled down his cheeks as he turned to King Tyburr. "Father, can't we just leave now? Aislin isn't going to come with me, and Gorinda's going to be so angry that we'll lose her protection."

"I don't know what you're talking about," King Tyburr said, looking horrified. "Hold your tongue, boy, before you spout any more foolish prattle."

"No!" said the fairy king. Although he kept his voice low, it had more power in it than the thunder rumbling outside. King Tyburr flinched and bowed his head.

"This boy interests me," King Darinar continued. "Let him tell us what he knows about this sorceress."

King Tyburr's head shot up. "There isn't one," he exclaimed. "Rory made her up to excuse his actions."

Queen Surinen leaned forward on her throne to stare into the human king's eyes. Her own eyes seemed to burn into him. "I used a truth spell on your son, so I know that he isn't lying. Must I use one on you as well?"

King Tyburr's face turned pale and he took a step back. "That would be unthinkable. I am a king. I would consider a spell like that an act of war if you even *try* to use it on me."

"That won't be necessary, my dear," King Darinar told his wife, setting his hand on top of hers. "I'm sure we can still learn much from Prince Rory."

The queen turned her gaze on Rory, which made him squirm and look away. "You're right," she said. "Prince Rory, describe Gorinda to me. What does she look like?"

Rory looked as if he'd tasted something bad and was about to spit, but all he finally said was, "I can't say. And now that I think hard about it, I can't even picture her in my mind."

Queen Surinen frowned. "Gorinda has used magic on him."

With a crook of her finger, she summoned one of her sprite attendants to her. A few whispered words and the little man darted off. He was back in less than a minute, holding a pouch to his chest. Handing it to the queen, he bowed and backed away. With deft fingers, the queen opened the pouch and removed a pinch of the dust inside. Holding it before her lips, she leaned toward Rory and blew gently. The dust puffed around him and seemed to disappear as it landed on his skin, his hair, and his clothes.

Rory looked relieved at first when nothing seemed to happen. But after a few seconds his entire body began to vibrate and give off a faint hum that set Aislin's teeth on edge even from across the room. Rory glanced down at himself in surprise.

Queen Surinen stood and stepped down from the raised dais to examine him more closely. As he began to turn a sickly shade of blue, with a darker color forming around his mouth, she nodded. "It seems that Gorinda has placed a geas on you, preventing you from talking about her. I believe she has also placed a compulsion on you to do something," she said as the color turned muddy green. "Turn your head and look at Aislin."

The queen pointed at Rory, then made a swooping gesture with her hand, causing him to turn so that he was facing Aislin. The green flared to a brighter shade and stayed that way until the fairy queen made him look away. "What's going on?" Rory asked in a strangled voice.

Queen Surinen climbed back up the dais to sit on her throne again. She studied Rory, looking more and more distressed as time passed. "The compulsion she placed on you was related to Aislin," the queen finally said. "More than likely it was to make you take Aislin from us. The compulsion won't go away if you leave here. If you were to return home, you would be back again and again until you succeeded. Even if you weren't guilty of trickery and attempted abduction, we couldn't let you go with your father, at least not until we learn who this Gorinda really is and what she has planned.

"As it is, Gorinda has layered spells over spells. I could hurt you if I were to remove them in the incorrect order, so at this point I don't dare try. Once I learn what kind of magic Gorinda uses, I should be able to ascertain what I need to do to counter it."

"But I swear I won't come near Aislin again!" protested Rory. "I just want to go home now."

"A compulsion is meant to make you do something whether you want to or not," said King Darinar. "Queen Surinen is right in saying that you must stay here for now. We have to keep an eye on you to make sure you don't act on the compulsion. And compulsion or not, you must be held accountable for your actions."

Queen Surinen nodded. "You trapped our fairies and attempted to kidnap our granddaughter. No one may do such things without consequences. For trapping my fairies, you must clean all the windows of the palace. And for the crime of treating my granddaughter as you did, you will be turned into a marmoset for as long as it takes you to clean the windows."

"What's a marmoset?" Kimble asked Poppy.

"A little kind of monkey," Poppy replied. "I think they're cute, but I wouldn't want to be one, especially not if I had to clean all those windows!"

"That human prince should be grateful that the queen didn't think of something more permanent," Deela added.

"But my son—" began King Tyburr.

"Will be safe here until he has served his sentence and we have removed the compulsion," King Darinar told him. "If you want him back, you must help us all you can. Do you know anything of this Gorinda? Have you ever met her or heard of her before now?"

King Tyburr sighed. "Yes, I know of the woman, but my kingdom's relationship with her is not a happy one and I had hoped not to make it public. Years ago, Gorinda came to my father and threatened to make our crops fail and our wells go dry if we didn't pay her a tithe every year. My father was weak. He feared the sorceress and paid the tithe year after year. On his deathbed, he made me promise that I would as well, saying that Morain was not strong enough to stand up to her. I'm ashamed to say that I continued what he had started without considering taking up arms against her. I didn't know how to fight her magic. When Aghamonda came to me, saying she could help me defeat the king of Scarmander, I foolishly thought to ask her to help us defeat Gorinda. But our conversation never reached that point."

"Have you ever met Gorinda?" asked Queen Surinen.

"No, I haven't," replied the king.

"Did you know that your son had met her?" King Darinar asked him.

King Tyburr shook his head. "I didn't know until I heard him speak of her just now. I thought he'd heard rumors and wanted to use them to invent an excuse for his behavior. Now I know that I was wrong. I'm sorry, Rory," he said to his son. "I should have believed you."

Rory shrugged and looked away.

"Do you have anything to say for yourself?" the fairy queen asked Rory.

The prince made a face, but once again the words

spilled out even when he fought to stay silent. "All I can say is that I wouldn't have tried to take Aislin the way I did if I'd known that I'd get caught. I would have tried something else then. I just don't know what it would have been."

"I like that truth spell!" Poppy whispered to her friends.

Aislin took a step forward. "If I may, Grandmother, I have something to say." When the queen nodded, Aislin turned to Rory. "You still seem to think that you don't have to be nice to people. I just want you to know that compulsion or not, whether you're talking about a fairy or a princess, there's never a good excuse to be unkind to anyone."

Queen Surinen nodded again. "Very true. And I want Prince Rory to think about that as he serves his sentence." Pointing her finger at Rory, she announced, "Your sentence begins now!" A ray of sparkling light shot from her finger and hit Prince Rory squarely on his chest. As the light engulfed him, he began to shrink. His clothes disappeared as he became covered in fur. Within moments, he was a monkey small enough to fit in Aislin's pocket.

King Darinar turned to one of the guards

standing at the side of the room. "Take Prince Rory to the kitchen and ask the scullery maids to give him soap and water so he may start washing the windows. Aislin, you and your mestari may go now. I'm sure you'd like to rest after your ordeal."

Aislin bowed to her grandparents and hurried from the room with her ladies in tow. "What I really want to do is take a bath," she told Poppy. "Knowing that Rory touched me makes my skin feel dirty."

"I don't blame you," said her friend. "I'll go ahead and get your bath ready." A moment later, Poppy turned tiny and darted down the corridor.

"I didn't like Prince Rory from the first time I saw him," Kimble proclaimed. "He gives me the heebie-jeebies."

"What does that mean?" asked Twinket.

"You know—he creeps me out big time," Kimble explained. "I wouldn't want him to touch me either."

"It's all my fault," Deela moaned. "I'll never leave you unprotected like that again, Your Highness."

"You heard Queen Surinen," said Aislin. "Rory is under a compulsion. He was going to keep trying until he succeeded. At least now we know what he was up to and who was behind it."

Tomas had been leaning against the wall, waiting for them. Spotting Aislin, he straightened up and said, "Aislin, may I speak to you alone?"

The princess glanced at her mestari. "You may go on ahead. I'm perfectly safe here in the palace. I'll be along in just a minute."

"But I don't think you should—"

"Please go," said Aislin.

Her mestari were still reluctant to leave, but once they did, Tomas took Aislin's hand and pulled her into an alcove where they were out of sight. "Are you all right?" he asked. "I heard about what Rory did. It's all anyone is talking about now. He didn't hurt you, did he?"

The princess shook her head. "He didn't," she said. "I'm fine."

"Because if he hurt you I would make him regret the day he was born," Tomas said, squeezing his free hand into a fist. "I would—"

"I really am fine," Aislin assured him. "You don't have to do anything to Rory. My grandmother turned him into a marmoset and he's going to be very busy washing the palace windows."

Tomas looked surprised when he said, "A

marmoset, huh? Well, good. But compulsion or not, if he ever so much as looks at you funny, I'm going to take him apart."

"I appreciate your concern, however I'm not a helpless maiden and I can take care of myself!" Aislin told him. "Rory may not realize it, but he has a lot more to fear from me than I do from him."

"I know that, but my offer still stands," Tomas said, and let go of her hand. "I may not be one of your mestari, but I am still your friend."

"One of my best," Aislin said, and gave him a grateful smile before turning and walking away.

The princess reached her bathing room a short time later to find that Poppy had already added rose petals and lavender to the water and placed clean clothes on the bed. Glancing down, Aislin found red marks on her arms where Rory had held her. Suddenly she was eager to undress, and when she stepped into the pool, she wasn't sure if she would ever want to wear her jade green gown again.

After scrubbing and rinsing herself three times, she washed her hair twice. She was contemplating washing it again when there was a knock on the door and Twinket peeked in. "I'm sorry to disturb you, but King Darinar and Queen Surinen request that you join them in the courtyard as soon as possible."

"I thought they said I could rest," said Aislin.

"I guess they changed their minds. The messenger said that it has something to do with Aghamonda."

Aislin frowned and reached for a towel. "I wonder what it could be now. They can't think that she's had anything to do with Rory. She's been a statue for weeks."

When Aislin arrived, the king and queen of the fairies were standing in front of the statue that dominated the courtyard. The king was scratching his chin, and the queen was tapping her cheek with one finger. Aislin thought they both looked worried.

They looked up as Aislin approached. "We've spoken to the human royals who are here at the palace," said Queen Surinen. "They all admit to paying tithes to Gorinda, although none of them seem to have met her. It occurred to me that if Rory used the same mist to put you to sleep that Aghamonda used on you,

Aghamonda might have met her and can describe her to us."

"How can you talk to a statue?" Aislin asked her.

"She won't be a statue when we question her," said the queen as she reached into a soft gold-colored bag. "This is the only thing that will release her from the spell. Stand back in case she falls down."

Opening the bag, Queen Surinen took out a small vial. Aghamonda was tall even for a fairy, so the queen had to stand on her tiptoes to pour one drop onto the statue's head as she murmured words too softly for anyone to hear. Almost instantly, the gray-white of the statue faded away, becoming the vibrant colors of a living fairy. Aghamonda gasped and staggered, catching herself before she could fall.

"What's happening?" she asked, her voice rough from disuse. "I feel so odd!"

"That will pass," said Queen Surinen. "We need you to answer a few questions."

"Why should I tell you anything if you're going to turn me back into a statue again?" asked Aghamonda.

"Because if you help us now, we might reduce your sentence," the king told her.

"What do you want to know?" Aghamonda said grudgingly.

"Do you know a sorceress named Gorinda?" asked the king.

The statue looked away as if she could no longer meet their eyes. "I know many sorceresses," said Aghamonda. "One may be named Gorinda."

"Is she the one who gave you the sleeping mist?" asked the queen.

"Maybe," Aghamonda replied. "Being a statue has made my memory foggy."

"If she gave you the sleeping mist, you must have seen her. What can you tell us about her?" Queen Surinen continued. Aghamonda's attitude seemed to annoy the queen whose tone was becoming more insistent.

Aghamonda sighed. "You aren't going to stop, are you? My head aches and you're making it worse with all your questions. I'll tell you what I can about Gorinda so you'll stop prattling on. She is a very powerful sorceress—with far stronger magic than either of you. She was kind to me when I needed kindness. Small-minded humans in a tiny village were tormenting me, and she came to my rescue. Gorinda was the one to teach me how to deal with humans when I had no other fairy friends or family to turn to. I will always be grateful to her and I won't betray her, even if you add many lifetimes to my sentence. Now turn me back if you're going to so I might have some peace."

"As you wish," said the queen, pointing at Agha-monda. A few soft words and a sprinkling of silver sparkles turned the fairy into a statue once again.

"Do you think Gorinda put a compulsion on her, too?" Aislin asked.

"No, even the most powerful sorceress cannot place a compulsion on a fairy," said King Darinar. "They must use other means to convince a fairy to do something. Sometimes kindness can be more convincing than cruelty. I'm not surprised that Agha-monda won't tell us about Gorinda if the sorceress was so good to her. We'll have to find another way to learn what we can about the woman behind all this."

Chapter 14

Aislin was restless that night and had a hard time falling asleep. When she did, images of Rory carrying her off to some faceless sorceress filled her dreams, waking her again. After tossing and turning for what seemed like hours, she finally drifted into a deeper rest, only to have Twinket jump on her chest to wake her.

"Wake up! Something terrible has happened!" the little doll shouted only inches from Aislin's face. "Aghamonda has escaped!"

"What?" Aislin cried, sitting up and dumping Twinket off her. "How did that happen?"

The princess scrambled out of bed and threw a

robe on over her nightgown. "No one knows," Twinket said. "She was just gone this morning, but there are scratch marks on the floor, so the queen thinks Aghamonda was still a statue when she left. Oh, and a couple of fairies were frozen. Queen Surinen hopes they'll be able to tell us what happened when they thaw out. She's working on that now."

"Where is Queen Surinen?" asked Aislin.

"Both of your grandparents are in the courtyard, looking for something that can tell us what happened. Hurry up! We're missing all sorts of important stuff."

Aislin and Twinket ran out the door and down the corridor. "Wake up!" Twinket yelled, pounding on the doors of Aislin's other ladies-in-waiting as she passed by. "Everybody needs to help!"

By the time they reached the courtyard, a small crowd had already gathered. Tomas was there along with his father. Human-sized fairies clustered together, whispering and looking around as if they expected Aghamonda to return at any moment, while tiny fairies fluttered nervously overhead. Fairy and pedrasi warriors stood at every corner of the courtyard, looking vigilant. Aislin nodded at Captain Larch and Kivi when she saw them. When she reached Tomas, she paused. "Why are you up so early? Were you summoned, too?"

"My father and I got up early to go fishing," Tomas replied. "This trip has turned into a vacation for us and we're having a great time, or at least we were until we heard the commotion and found out that Aghamonda had escaped. Now everyone is afraid and doesn't know what to do. Your grandparents are still trying to find out what happened."

Aislin glanced at her grandmother, who was gesturing at her to come over. "I have to go. I'll talk to you later," she told Tomas.

The princess approached three ashen-faced fairies wrapped in soft, warm blankets. "Were you the fairies who were frozen?" she asked them.

Lilac nodded, making her springy purple curls bounce. "It was awful! We were minding our own business, taking a shortcut through the courtyard, when we heard this terrible grinding sound. You're probably used to it, being part pedrasi and all, but I'd never heard a sound like that before."

Potentilla shivered. "We didn't know what it was

at first, so we all looked over there," she said, pointing, "and saw the statue of Aghamonda—"

"It *was* Aghamonda, silly!" said Zinnia. "She was walking across the stone floor, and her feet were making the sound with every step she took. It was truly terrifying!"

"She didn't look our way, but Hydrangea was hovering over her and she saw us. That nasty little wisp pointed at us and cast a freezing spell." Lilac shivered at the thought. "And to think that she used to be my best friend!"

"Do you think Hydrangea freed Aghamonda from your spell?" Aislin asked Queen Surinen.

Aislin's grandmother nodded at the three fairies and they scurried off, still clutching their blankets. "It looks that way," the queen replied. "She left after she freed Aghamonda and froze the fairies. No one has seen her since."

"From the evidence we've found, Hydrangea must have been spying on us when Queen Surinen removed the spell to allow us to question Aghamonda," said the king.

"Hydrangea must have seen what vial I used, but she couldn't hear the words I said. The drop of my potion and the words I spoke must take place simultaneously, or they won't remove the spell completely. Without those words, all Hydrangea could do was allow Aghamonda to move, but she'll remain a statue and be unable to use her magic."

"Why would Hydrangea want to do that?" asked Aislin.

"She probably thought that the drop of potion was all she needed," said Queen Surinen. "I say the words under my breath on purpose so no one else will know them. What I don't understand is why Hydrangea would do such a thing. She never seemed rebellious before."

"I might know why," Aislin told her. "Hydrangea was upset that I didn't choose her as one of my mestari. I had hoped she'd gotten over it, but it's possible that she was still mad. I'm so sorry. This may be my fault."

Aislin felt guilty. She'd expected some attitude from the fairies she hadn't chosen, but nothing like this! She frowned and ran her fingers through her hair, wishing she'd kept a better eye on Hydrangea.

"Don't blame yourself. I'm sure Hydrangea didn't come up with this on her own," said the queen. "I wouldn't be surprised if the sorceress Gorinda had something to do with it. No one else has gone against us the way she has for a very long time. Whoever is behind all this, your grandfather and I need to look into it. We were just saying—"

A tiny fairy flew into the courtyard and headed straight for Captain Larch. A moment later, the captain of the palace guards hurried to the king and queen. "Our warriors patrolling the forest around the palace perimeter have reported that someone is shooting darts at all flying fairies, regardless of whether they're using their own wings or riding on the back of a bird or insect. Three of our warriors have been injured. I've sent the order that all patrols be performed on foot, which greatly limits our ability to keep everyone safe."

"I understand," King Darinar replied. "No fairy should turn small and fly outside until we find out what's going on. And I don't want anyone leaving the palace unless it's absolutely necessary. If Gorinda is behind this, things will probably get worse until she's stopped. We need to locate her as soon as we can." The faces of the fairies in the room had all gone pale. Fairies were vulnerable when they were tiny. The thought that anyone might deliberately hurt them then was unbearable. Although Aislin didn't think she could help find the assailants, something else was weighing on her mind.

"Did anyone see which way Aghamonda and Hydrangea headed?" asked Aislin.

"The statue's footprints headed east, deeper into the forest," Captain Larch replied.

"Baibre lives in that direction!" Aislin exclaimed. "Someone needs to go warn her."

King Darinar shook his head. "No one is leaving the palace until we can assure their safety. Captain, I want you to double the patrol to make up for the lack of our eyes in the sky. I don't want any more of our fairies to be injured, so have them wear their armor and travel in pairs."

Captain Larch bowed his head to the king and hurried from the courtyard. When the king and queen started talking to each other in low voices, Aislin turned and headed out as well. Tomas stepped in front of her before she could leave. "I heard what you said about Baibre," he said quietly. "I know you well enough to guess that you have something in mind."

"You heard King Darinar. No one is allowed to leave the palace," Aislin told him. She gave Tomas a meaningful look, then pointedly glanced at the fairy king.

"Ah," said Tomas. "I'll see you soon."

As Aislin left the courtyard, her mestari followed her. "You're up to something, aren't you?" Poppy whispered to Aislin as they hurried down the corridor.

"Baibre told me how vengeful Aghamonda can be and she might be in real danger! We have to tell Baibre that her sister is headed her way," Aislin whispered in reply. "It's partly my fault that they got back together in the first place. We have to hurry though. It won't take long before word spreads that we aren't allowed outside and the guards will try to stop us. Please tell the other mestari that we'll be leaving in five minutes."

They ran to their rooms to dress in the tunics and leggings that Sage and Parsley had made for them. Aislin made sure that Sage had hidden a diamond in her tunic, just in case. She noticed that someone had brought her a basket of pastries while she was in the courtyard. Grabbing the knapsack she'd taken into Mount Gora, she dumped its contents on her bed, planning to leave behind anything she didn't really need. She found the hardtack and the packet of dried berries that she'd never opened and stuffed them back in. After filling the gourd with fresh water, she put that in as well. She hesitated when she found the calcite globe, then put it back in; it might be useful someday. After wrapping the pastries in the cloth that had lined the basket, she tucked them in and was ready to go.

Her mestari were waiting for her in the corridor. They practically ran through the palace to the door that opened onto the crystal bridge. No one was in sight as they slipped out of the palace and hurried down the bridge. It wasn't until they reached the forest that Aislin began to think that they might get away unnoticed.

They made their way through the forest, keeping an eye out for patrolling warriors and dart-wielding strangers, and suddenly they heard the whinny of a fairy-bred horse. Aislin had ridden such a horse only once, but she had grown up around them and recognized the distinctive sound. She stopped moving and her ladies did, too. Knowing that fairies on patrol didn't use horses, Aislin couldn't imagine who was riding through the forest. She was startled when Tomas, the pedrasi named Kivi, and the fairy Sycamore stepped out from behind some pine trees leading seven fairy steeds.

"When you left the courtyard so abruptly, your grandparents were sure you'd try something like this," Tomas told her. "They know how determined you can be. They also know how well you can take care of yourself, especially with the ladies you chose. Sycamore and Kivi are supposed to go with you and I invited myself along. We're riding so we can get there and back as quickly as possible."

"My mestari are already helping me," Aislin told the two fairy guards.

"We understand, Your Highness," said Sycamore. "We wouldn't dream of interfering. We're just here to assist if you need us."

"In that case, you are welcome to join us," Aislin replied.

Kimble held up her hand and waved it in the air. "Uh, I've never ridden a horse before."

"I have," said Deela. "You can ride with me."

"Anyone else never ridden before?" asked Kivi.

Although Poppy looked uncomfortable, she didn't say anything. "Poppy and Twinket can go with me," Aislin announced. She remembered how much Poppy had hated it the one time she'd tried to ride a horse by herself. Poppy gave her a grateful look and a half smile. It would make them both feel better to have the other one there.

A few minutes later they were all astride their horses, with Kimble sitting in front of Deela and Aislin sandwiched between Twinket and Poppy. "There's an extra horse," said Twinket.

"We'll take it with us. Baibre can ride it if she decides to come back to the palace," Sycamore replied before turning to Aislin. "I understand that you know the way to her home."

"Tomas and I both do," the princess replied. "We'll have to head east for a while."

"It would take us days to get there by foot," said Tomas. "But nothing takes long when you ride one of these beauties." He leaned over to pat the neck of the fairy horse he was riding. The steed shook his head and flicked his ears as if a fly was bothering him, but it didn't make a sound.

Fairy horses don't make any noise unless they want to, so the party sped silently through the forest while their riders kept watch for Aghamonda. Grazing deer looked up, startled. A wild boar rooting through the underbrush with her babies grunted when the horses surprised her. When the fairy horses passed a unicorn drinking from a stream, it looked up so quickly that water streamed from its mouth. The unicorn ran with them for a time, keeping pace with the fairy horses until it began to tire.

When they finally reached the road and headed south, the horses were able to pick up speed. They crossed a bridge over a rushing river, surprising two gnomes fishing on the riverbank. Less than an hour later, Aislin spotted a set of rocks shaped like a sleeping cat. "Anyone who is carrying a weapon either has to leave it here or stay behind and wait for us," she told the others.

"I don't like that," said Deela. "How can we protect you then?"

"Baibre cast a spell on this forest a long time ago," Aislin told her. "No one carrying weapons can find her home. The only way we'll reach her is if you leave your weapons behind. Otherwise we could wander around in this forest for hours."

"Which isn't fun, believe me," Tomas said, shaking his head.

"Maybe one of us should stay and guard the weapons," suggested Lin.

"That's a good idea," said Kivi. "Any volunteers?"

They all looked at each other, waiting for someone to step forward, but no one did. "Oh, all right," said Twinket. "I'll do it."

Sycamore laughed. "I think we need someone who can *use* a weapon."

"Why don't we just hide them?" asked Aislin. "Can't one of you fairies use a spell so that no one will see them or step on them or something?"

"Why didn't I think of that?" said Poppy. "Put all your weapons under this tree. I'll make sure no one will touch them."

Deela was reluctant to set down her curved, barbed sword, but after she did, Lin placed her war hammer beside it. The others followed their example, and soon they were all weaponless. Aislin was surprised by how many they had been carrying. Even Kimble had been carrying a tiny crossbow and darts.

"Where did you get those?" Aislin asked Twinket when the doll laid some sharp sewing needles stuck in a scrap of cloth on the ground.

"I took them when Parsley wasn't looking," Twinket confessed. "I thought they'd be good for poking people."

Aislin was amused, but Poppy looked horrified.

"Remind me to never make you angry," she told the doll.

"I wouldn't poke you, Poppy," said Twinket. "I like you too much for that."

"How about that spell," Tomas reminded Poppy.

"Oh, right!" she said, and pointed her finger at the weapons. A patch of thistles sprang up over the weapons, concealing them from prying eyes and forming a barrier that no one would want to touch.

"We're looking for a waterfall," Aislin said as they mounted their horses again and started walking them between the trees. "It isn't very big, but we'll hear it before we see it."

They soon encountered a well-defined path, assuring Aislin that they were going the right way. Poppy, Aislin, and Sycamore heard the sound of the waterfall before the others; the rest of their party heard it minutes later. It wasn't long before they came upon the small lake beneath the falls.

"How far away is Baibre's home?" Deela asked.

"It's right there," Aislin said, looking up. "It's bigger than it was when Tomas and I were here."

"I'll say!" exclaimed Tomas.

The treehouse that had filled the upper branches

of one tree now extended to two more huge trees, creating an impressive silhouette in the forest canopy. Birds flew in and out of the open windows, twittering madly as they shared the news that the princess was back. Everyone dismounted, leaving the fairy horses to wait patiently for their return.

When Aislin walked around one of the trees, the rest of her party followed. On the other side of the massive trunk, they found Baibre's manticore curled up on the doorstep. Yawning, the great beast got to its lion paws so it could bow to the princess. Kimble gasped when she saw the three rows of teeth in its human-looking head.

"Welcome back," the manticore said to Aislin. "Baibre is waiting for you."

He stepped aside to let her pass. Twinket, Poppy, and Tomas hurried after her, but when Deela tried to follow, the manticore slunk in front of her and growled. "No orcs allowed," he said. "And the rest of you can't go in either. It's a treehouse, not a fairy palace."

Aislin stopped to glance back at her friends. "We won't be long," she told them.

The steps inside the tree trunk were too high for Twinket, so Aislin had to carry her to the top.

Reaching the last step, the princess saw Baibre and an older fairy couple waiting with smiles on their faces. The griffin she had met during her last visit was there, too, perched on a bench made from logs.

"Welcome to our home!" Baibre cried. "Don't you just love what we did to it? My parents had a lot of great ideas."

"It looks wonderful," Aislin replied, looking around. The space was even bigger and airier than it had been before, with more branches holding up the longer ceiling and lots of walls in unexpected places. It was noisier, too, with even more birds and squirrels making their homes inside.

"I don't think you've ever met my parents," said Baibre. "This is my mother, Dewdrop, and my father, Branch."

"It's an honor to meet you, Your Highness!" Dewdrop gushed, curtseying to Aislin.

The fairy woman appeared to be only a few years older than Baibre, with an unlined face and silky blue hair trailing past her waist. The fairy man looked much older, as if he'd never used magic to keep himself looking young. "Hello!" he said, his gaze traveling from Aislin to Poppy.

When his eyes rested on Twinket and Tomas, he smiled again and added, "You have interesting traveling companions, Your Highness. Are you human?" he asked Tomas.

"I am," said Tomas.

"This is my friend Tomas," Aislin hurried to say. "He's the son of Duke Fadding, the heir to the throne of Scarmander. And these are Twinket and Poppy, two of my mestari."

"I'm an honorable mestari," Twinket said, looking proud.

"I'm sure you are," Branch said with a sparkle in his eyes. "Are you sightseeing? This forest is just as beautiful as when we used to live here."

"Actually, we've come with some bad news. Aghamonda has escaped the palace and is headed this way. A fairy used a spell that allowed your daughter to move, even though she's still a statue," Aislin said, her worried gaze going from one fairy to the other. "I came to warn you in case she plans to come here."

Dewdrop's face turned pale and she reached out to clutch her husband's arm. "We spoke to Aghamonda right before Queen Surinen turned her into a statue. Our daughter wasn't at all happy with us. She accused us of abandoning her when we moved and said she'd get even one day. We never meant to leave our girls. We'd thought they'd gone on ahead."

"She's mad at me, too," admitted Baibre. "She kidnapped me so she could take my magic from me. I really told her off. We had a big fight inside that locket and she's bound to come after me now."

"Why would a fairy free her like that?" asked Dewdrop. "I'd guess it was one of her friends, but she never had any, at least none that I ever met."

"We think a sorceress named Gorinda was behind it, but we don't know that for certain," Aislin told them. "We don't know anything about Gorinda, including what she looks like and where we might be able to find her."

With an earsplitting squawk, the griffin raised its eagle wings, launching itself into the air and out the largest window.

"We can't stay here," Branch told his wife and daughter. "Even if we use our magic to protect ourselves, Aghamonda is clever. She'd find some way to break through our defenses."

"Then you should head back to the palace," said Aislin. "You can return here after King Darinar and

Queen Surinen have Aghamonda in custody again. I'm sure it won't be long."

"The queen won't mind?" asked Dewdrop. "We wouldn't want to impose."

"She won't mind at all," Aislin told her. "And the sooner you go, the better."

Chapter 15

BAIBRE AND HER PARENTS hurriedly packed the few
things they were taking with them. Their possessions
were too heavy for them to carry when they were tiny,
so they'd have to be full-sized to return to Fairengar.

"It's just as well," Aislin told them as they
descended the stairs single file. "Someone is shooting
darts at the fairies who fly anywhere near the palace."

"That's horrible!" cried Dewdrop as she stepped
out of the tree trunk. "Why would anyone do that?"

"We don't know," said Sycamore. "But I'm sure
Captain Larch is doing his best to find out."

Aislin waited until they were all outside before
saying, "Everyone, this is Baibre and her parents,

Dewdrop and Branch." Glancing at her friends, she added, "These are my mestari, Deela, Lin, and Kimble. Sycamore and Kivi are both in the palace guard."

Baibre blushed when she said hello to Sycamore.

"We'll have to double up on the horses," Sycamore announced. "Your parents may ride the black gelding. Baibre, you may ride behind me."

From the look he and Baibre shared, Aislin guessed that they had met before.

Neither Dewdrop nor Branch had ever ridden a horse, so Kivi gave them a few quick instructions. As the party set off through the forest, the pedrasi guard kept his horse beside theirs to answer their questions. Aislin guided her horse to run next to the mare that Deela and Kimble were riding. "Have you seen any sign of the manticore or the griffin? I'm surprised they didn't come with us."

"When the griffin came out of the treehouse, it took off into the forest with the manticore," Deela replied.

"We haven't seen either one since," Kimble told her.

"That's odd," said Aislin. "They've sworn to protect Baibre and usually follow her everywhere."

The princess kept expecting the two creatures to return, but neither had shown up before the party reached the sleeping cat rocks. While Poppy pointed at the thistles, which turned brown and wilted to the ground, Kivi slipped off his horse. The pedrasi guard handed everyone's weapons to them, then they all returned to the road. When Tomas urged his horse to run next to Aislin's, Twinket grinned at him. They went faster, and were making good time when they approached the river they had crossed before. In the short time that they were gone, someone or something had destroyed the bridge, leaving piles of rubble on both sides of the churning water.

"Who do you think did that?" Poppy asked Aislin.

"Oh, dear!" Twinket cried, wringing her little cloth hands. "I have a bad feeling about this!"

There was a roar and the rubble exploded outward, showering rock onto the road and creating geysers in the river. One smaller rock hit Kivi, knocking him off his horse, which reared up and struck out with its hooves. The horse that Dewdrop and Branch were riding was too close and received a glancing blow from a hoof. Dumping its riders, their horse joined the black gelding and took off along the riverbank.

Kivi staggered when he got to his feet, favoring one of his legs as he went to help the two older fairies.

Aislin was so concerned about Baibre's parents and Kivi that she didn't notice the real problem until Twinket started screaming, "Don't let them rip off my arm again!" The doll clutched her repaired cloth arm to her chest, shivering.

Aislin's head whipped around. Trolls that had been hiding under the rubble lumbered up from the edge of the river, their eyes gleaming as they gnashed their teeth. It was hard to count them when they rushed toward her party roaring, but she thought there were at least a dozen. Deela, Lin, and Sycamore were the first to dismount and they stood with their legs braced, weapons ready. Then Kimble appeared, clutching her crossbow.

"We eat you!" screamed one of the trolls, and the others roared in agreement.

Tomas helped Poppy and Aislin dismount. While Aislin tried to decide what she could do to hold off the trolls, Poppy thrust her hand out, flinging her own kind of magic at the trolls. Weedy vines grew up around the trolls' ankles, snagging them and making them trip. Stinging wasps converged on the trolls, but their stingers were unable to pierce the thick, gray-green skin that was exposed through ragged clothes.

The trolls ignored the insects and didn't even bother swatting at them. Those who had been in the back stepped on the trolls that had fallen and were still struggling to get up. No troll was down for long, though, and within moments Lin was pounding them with her war hammer while Deela, Sycamore, and Tomas slashed at the trolls with their swords. Kimble had her little crossbow out and was carefully choosing her shots, aiming for the trolls' faces whenever possible. When she hit one between the eyes, he went cross-eyed and ran off, howling.

Aislin didn't notice when the manticore and the griffin returned, but then they were there, lunging and snapping while trying to keep the trolls away from the spot where Baibre and her parents were huddled together behind the remaining horses. "Fly away!" Aislin shouted to the three fairies. "Leave while you can."

"What about you?" asked Branch. "We can't just leave you."

"Go! I don't have time to argue," Aislin cried as she turned back to the battle.

Despite the valiant efforts of her friends, Aislin

knew that there was little they could do that would have much effect against the trolls. The last time trolls had come after them, Aislin and her party had had to run away. *But that was before I knew what I could do,* she thought.

Tapping into the strength of the diamond in her tunic and the gravel under her feet, Aislin threw up her arm, pulling the stones from the river's shores to pummel the trolls. The larger rocks brought the trolls to their knees, but they shook them off and kept coming. She drew sand from the riverbed, forming the sand leopards that had worked so well against human troops, but the trolls walked through them as if they weren't there.

Spotting the princess, the trolls grinned and fought to reach her. "We eat you first!" one bellowed.

Bracing herself, Aislin drew more power from the ground. The trolls were rushing toward her when she shifted the gravel beneath them, making it roil and churn so it was impossible for them to keep their footing. Farther down the riverbank, Lin closed in, swinging her war hammer with such force that it knocked a troll off his feet. Kivi followed her example to take down another troll, while Deela darted into the fray, dispatching the downed trolls with her barbed sword. Tomas and Sycamore used their swords to attack the trolls who got away from the mestari.

The roar of the trolls and the battle cries of her companions were deafening. Aislin was so caught up in what was going on around her that she didn't look away until the ground began to shake under the combatants' feet. All eyes turned to the far side of the river where trees swayed and fell, snapped in two or smashed into splinters as something big, angry, and determined came their way.

The trolls seemed confused as whatever was coming drew nearer, leaving a trail of broken trees in its wake. Aislin's companions looked fearful, however, especially when Sycamore shouted, "They've got reinforcements!"

"No," said Aislin, "I don't think so."

The devastation was heading directly toward them in a way that Aislin had seen before. Once, when she was a little girl and playing with her friends, another little girl had cut her foot on a sharp rock. She wailed, and her mother, who was never far off, came running. It's what giants did when a friend or loved one needed them.

"That's *our* reinforcement," Aislin said as fourteen-foot-tall Salianne came into view.

Tomas's eyes were wide when he said, "You're kidding, right?"

The girl giant had been one of Aislin and Poppy's closest friends when they were growing up. Although Aislin had been disappointed when she learned that Salianne wasn't going to be one of her mestari, she hadn't been surprised; the girl's parents were over-protective even when everything was normal. Aislin also knew that her giant friend was very strong-willed and usually got what she wanted. Salianne must have convinced her parents to let her come.

The princess was delighted to see her, especially now. The manticore, the griffin, and the fairy horses weren't happy about it, though. Terrified, most of the remaining horses raced off into the forest. The only one that stayed behind, pawing the ground and shaking her head, was the mare that Aislin had ridden. Twinket was standing on the horse's back, pulling on the reins and shouting, "Whoa!"

When Aislin noticed that the griffin and the

manticore had turned toward Salianne, bristling, she knew they saw the giant girl as a threat. "No!" Aislin shouted at the two beasts before they could launch an attack. Remembering to put power into her voice, she added, "She's a friend."

Both the manticore and the griffin looked at her as if she was crazy, but they stayed back as Salianne approached the river. The trolls had gathered at the edge of the water. Waving their arms in the air and screaming, "You not get us!" and "We eat you, too!" they paced back and forth on the riverbank as if afraid to get their feet wet.

Salianne didn't hesitate when she reached the river. With a roar that made the trolls sound like twittering birds, she leaped halfway across the river and landed in the water with a tremendous splash, creating a wave big enough to wash away the trolls closest to the river's edge. The giant girl disappeared for a moment, only to reappear much closer. Aislin and Salianne had taken lessons from the local water nymphs together, so the princess knew that the giantess could swim. She wasn't surprised when, with one sure stroke, her friend cut through the water and stood up, towering over the four-foot-tall trolls.

The trolls craned their necks back to look up as Salianne bent down and screamed in their faces, "You leave my friends alone!" The force of the air from her lungs knocked four trolls flat on their backs. The others cowered when Salianne picked up a troll with each hand. Twirling them over her head, she let go so that they flew off over the tops of trees, shrieking. Aislin didn't see where they landed, but she knew it was a long way away.

The remaining trolls watched, seemingly paralyzed, until Salianne turned back to them. She grabbed another when he started to run. When she threw him and he disappeared like the first two, the rest of the trolls tore into the forest, still wailing.

Salianne looked as if she was about to follow them until Aislin called out, "You needn't bother! I don't think we'll ever see those trolls again."

"I hate trolls," Salianne said, shading her eyes with one hand as she gazed after them. "They're nasty and rude and smell really, really bad. Papa says they can't help it, but being kind is a choice that anyone can make and if they don't want to stink, they should try bathing sometime. How are you, Aislin? They didn't hurt you, did they?" The giant girl strode back to

Aislin and bent down so that her eyes were level with the princess's.

"Oh, Salianne, I've missed you!" Aislin cried, throwing her arms around her friend's neck.

Up close, the giantess's freckles were as big as platters. Now that she had bent down, her braided brown hair shot with green fell over her shoulders to drag on the ground. Salianne's green eyes sparkled as she patted Aislin on the back as gently as she could.

It felt to Aislin as if someone was pummeling her with a sack of flour. She wondered if she'd have bruises. But she knew Salianne meant well. "I'm fine," she told her friend. "Thank you for coming when you did. I'm glad your parents let you join me. They do know you're here, don't they?"

"They gave me their permission to go to the palace," Salianne replied. "They don't know that I went there and found out you were gone. As far as I'm concerned, they'll never know that I followed you here."

"You threw trolls!" Twinket cried. "That was so cool!"

"Hi, Twinket!" Salianne said, grinning. "I haven't seen either of you in ages. Is that Poppy over there? What fun!"

"I hate to interrupt, but we should probably go. Those trolls may well come back," said Tomas.

Aislin glanced at the forest where the trolls had disappeared, then at the girl giant. "I don't think so," she said. "Not as long as Salianne is with us. Everyone, this is Salianne, one of my best friends and my newest mestari."

When Aislin introduced her to the other ladies, Salianne listened attentively to their names. She was most interested in Deela and Kimble, however. "I've never met an orc girl before. And what are you?" she asked Kimble.

"I'm a spriggan," Kimble replied. "I come from Mount Gora."

"What's he?" Salianne asked, looking at Tomas. "Is he part pedrasi and part fairy like you?"

"I'm human," he told her. "My name is Tomas. It's a pleasure to meet you."

"Is it?" said Salianne. "Is that because I'm a giant?"

Tomas shook his head. "No, it's because you're one of Aislin's friends."

Aislin was introducing the two guards to Salianne when Baibre and her parents darted back. They landed beside Sycamore and well away from the giantess before turning big again. When Baibre started talking to the griffin and the manticore, Aislin couldn't help but listen.

"Where were you?" Baibre asked them. "I expected you to come with us, but I didn't see you anywhere."

"Birdbrain heard the princess talking about a sorceress named Gorinda," said the manticore. "When Princess Aislin said that she didn't know much about the sorceress, we went to ask around. We found out some stuff, but none of it is good."

The griffin squawked and shook his feathered head while twitching his lion's tail.

"What did you learn?" Aislin asked the manticore.

"An eagle told us that someone named Gorinda has moved into the top of a mountain to the east. He said that weird stuff has been happening there, so he and his mate moved their nest. He said that you shouldn't go anywhere near it."

"I appreciate your eagle friend's warning, but that is precisely where we need to go," said Aislin.

"I don't think that's a good idea, Your Highness," Sycamore told her. "We should all return to the palace and tell King Darinar and Queen Surinen what we've learned."

Aislin shook her head. "I don't see any reason why

I should return to the palace now. We're already part-way to the mountain. Kimble, Deela, Lin, and I know mountains better than anyone at the palace. No, we're heading there now."

The spriggan girl nodded enthusiastically and seemed proud that the princess had included her. "If someone is in a mountain, we'll find them like that!" she said, snapping her fingers.

"I do think *you* need to return to the palace," Aislin told Sycamore. "You may escort Baibre and her parents, then inform the king and queen of what we've learned. If you fly most of the way, you'll get there much faster than I would. The horses have run off with Baibre's family's possessions, so you have no reason to stay this size now."

"Your grandparents won't like that I left you to face Gorinda unprotected," Sycamore said.

"I won't be unprotected," Aislin replied. "I'll have my mestari with me."

"They fight just as well as, if not better than, most warriors," said Kivi. "I plan to tell everyone I know about the strength and fierceness of the princess's mestari."

"Good," Aislin told him. "I want people to know just how good they are."

241

"Even so . . ." Sycamore began.

"Kivi can go with us, too," Aislin added, glancing at the pedrasi guard. "He can't fly, so he would hold you back."

"Uh, I might hold you back, too," Kivi told her. He pointed at his now obviously swollen ankle that he'd hurt when his horse threw him.

"I can take care of that," Aislin said. "Sit down and let me examine it."

Kivi gave her a funny look, but he sat on the closest boulder and stuck out his foot. When Aislin sat down beside him, he moved over a few inches and shifted his foot closer to her. Setting her hand on his ankle, Aislin closed her eyes and reached into the stone with her mind, drawing up power and sending it into the injured ankle. She could feel the swelling diminish under her hand as well as sense it in her mind. When all the swelling was gone and the damage that had caused it repaired, she sat back and opened her eyes.

"It feels great now!" Kivi said, turning his foot from side to side.

Salianne gasped. "I knew your mama was teaching you how to heal people, but that was amazing!"

"I've been working on a lot of things since the last time I saw you," Aislin told her.

"I really think you should go back with me," Sycamore began.

Aislin didn't have the time or the patience to argue with him, so she did something she didn't like doing to friends—she drew power into her voice and commanded him. "Go to the palace without me."

Sycamore looked annoyed, but he bowed and said, "I'll rejoin you once I've delivered Baibre's family to the palace and made my report to King Darinar and Queen Surinen. Torren's Peak is the only mountain of any size to the east. I'll look for you there."

"Wonderful," Aislin replied, already feeling sorry for using power on him. "Thank you."

She noticed that Baibre was talking to the manticore and the griffin again, but this time she didn't hear what the fairy told them. She did notice, however, that the two beasts remained behind when the fairies became small and flew off.

"We have one horse left," Tomas said. "How are we going to work this?"

"Baibre told us to stay and help you," said the manticore. "Birdbrain and I can each carry someone."

"So can I," said Salianne. "But I'd prefer to carry someone I know. I'll carry you and Twinket, Aislin."

"Perfect!" said Aislin.

"I can fly," said Poppy. "I'll scout ahead for danger."

Aislin looked at her for a moment before nodding. "All right, but promise me that if you see anything unusual, you'll come straight back."

"I promise," said Poppy.

When they finally started back up the road, Salianne was carrying Tomas as well as Aislin and Twinket, Kivi and Lin were on horseback, Deela rode astride the manticore, and Kimble was hiding her face behind the griffin's feathered head, too afraid to look down. Poppy spent the first few minutes flying circles around them before she left.

"I hope I didn't make a big mistake by letting her fly ahead," Aislin said as she watched her fairy friend go.

"Poppy will be fine," Tomas told her. "She's the one with fairy magic, remember?"

Chapter 16

THEY WERE WELL PAST the sleeping cat rocks when Aislin turned to Tomas. "I wonder why there were so many trolls by that bridge. I've never seen or heard of more than three or four traveling together. More than that and they usually get into terrible fights and no one walks away."

"That's a good point," Tomas replied. "Something must have drawn them there."

"I see a lake up ahead," Salianne told them. "Do you mind if we stop for a drink? I'm parched."

It was a warm day and they had yet to rest after setting out that morning. "Great idea," said Aislin. "I'm sure everyone could use a drink. Just let Poppy check the water first to make sure it's okay. I don't think we can take anything for granted now."

"Hey, Poppy!" Salianne yelled in a voice that made everyone within a mile turn and look her way.

Poppy came darting back, a worried expression on her face. "Is everything all right?" she asked.

"Yeah," said Salianne. "I just want to get a drink from that lake. Could you see if the water is all right?"

"You didn't have to yell for that!" Poppy told her. "I could hear you just fine when you used your regular voice. Everything you say carries a really long way."

"Then maybe I should whisper," the giantess whispered.

Poppy sighed. "That's still really loud."

"We have a giant with us," Kimble announced. "We won't be sneaking up on anyone."

"When you have a giant with you, you don't need to be sneaky," Salianne boasted.

"That's true," Twinket said. "And I like it!"

"I'll check the water," Poppy told them, and flew off.

Salianne's stride was so long that they reached the lake in less than a minute. The giantess knelt at the shoreline and set Tomas, Aislin, and Twinket on the ground beside her. A circle of water still sparkled from Poppy's spell. "It's fine to drink," the fairy said as she landed and grew big again. "And great to swim in if you want to cool off."

When the others showed up, Poppy was already wading knee-deep in the water and Salianne was scooping up great handfuls and drinking noisily. Aislin and Tomas took off their shoes while Twinket began to collect dandelion blossoms to make wreaths for all the ladies. Deela dismounted from the manticore and patted his shoulder. "Thank you for the ride. Who would have thought that riding on a manticore's back would be so comfortable?"

"You're welcome," the manticore replied. "Who would have thought that orcs could be so polite?"

While the beast padded down to the water to drink, Deela strolled over to see what the others were doing. "If you're going swimming, you can count me out. Orcs don't float. Our bodies are so dense that we sink right to the bottom."

"You can wade though, can't you?" Lin said as she and Kivi led the fairy horse to the water to drink. "Pedrasi sink, too, but I'm going to walk out as far as I can to cool off. Getting my clothes wet will keep me cooler while they dry."

"I suppose I could do that," Deela said, glancing

247

at the water warily. "I've never been in water deeper than a bathtub before."

"Look at me!" Kimble shouted. She had already jumped into the water and was paddling back and forth past Poppy.

While Kivi, Lin, and Deela waded close to shore, Kimble swam at the edge of the deeper water. Poppy tried to swim with her, but fairies are so light that they float even if they try to swim under the surface. When Kimble discovered this, she dove under Poppy and grabbed the fairy, pulling her down and letting her go so that the fairy shot up to the surface like a cork. Every time this happened, Poppy shrieked and got a mouthful of water.

After Kimble had pulled Poppy under the third time, the fairy announced, "I'll see if I can find some berries," and swam back to shore.

Kimble was watching Poppy swim away when the little spriggan girl suddenly gasped and disappeared under water. Aislin laughed, expecting Kimble to reappear any second, but as time passed, she began to be concerned.

"How long can a spriggan hold her breath?" she asked, scanning the water.

"I have no idea," Tomas replied. "I didn't even know that spriggans existed until I met Kimble."

Worried, Aislin pulled off her shoes and ran into the water. Taking a deep breath, she went under to see if she could spot Kimble. The lake was clear near the surface but got murkier in its depths. When she couldn't see the spriggan anywhere, she really began to worry. She dove, finally spotting something below her.

It's a kelpi, she thought, and realized that it was dragging Kimble deeper into the water, her limp little body flopping from its mouth.

Aislin knew about kelpis, although she hadn't seen one in a very long time. They looked like horses, but they weren't anything like them. Nasty and deceitful, they usually sought their prey on land, where they lured innocents onto their backs. Once seated on a kelpi, its victim was unable to dismount and couldn't escape when the beast dove into deep water. Both her father and King Darinar had banned kelpis from the land between the mountains, sending their warriors to drive them out. Finding them here shouldn't have been a surprise.

Although Aislin would have loved to use power in her voice to tell the kelpi to let the spriggan go, she didn't have enough air in her lungs to do it. There was a *boom* and a sudden change in the water pressure made Aislin glance back. The fairy horse that Kivi and Lin had been riding was heading straight toward the kelpi.

Aislin stayed back as the fairy horse plunged past her, its legs churning the water and creating a current of their own. Reaching the kelpi, the horse bit the back of the beast's neck, drawing blood. When the kelpi opened its mouth to scream, it let go of Kimble. The fairy horse slammed into the kelpi and shoved its own head under Kimble. While the kelpi swam away as fast as it could, the fairy horse lifted the spriggan to the surface. Aislin followed, gasping for air when she could finally breathe again. The fairy horse paused long enough for her to grab onto its mane. Grateful for its help, Aislin let the horse drag her toward shore.

Everyone was waiting on shore, with the manticore pacing back and forth behind them. Aislin hadn't quite reached the water's edge when Tomas waded out to help her. Seeing Kimble, he took the spriggan from the fairy horse and carried her to the grass. The spriggan girl's lips were blue and she didn't seem to be breathing when Aislin knelt beside her.

"Is she going to be all right?" asked Salianne.

"She is if I can help it," Aislin replied. All she had

wanted to do was help her fairy grandparents with the move and to keep everyone safe. Putting anyone in danger was the last thing she'd wanted. If she couldn't help this one friend, she'd feel like an absolute failure.

Setting her hands on Kimble's chest, Aislin closed her eyes and drew on the power in the diamond. At first she didn't detect any sign of life, but when she found the faintest beat of the girl's heart, Aislin knew that she had a chance. After rolling Kimble onto her side, Aislin used her healing powers to draw the water out of the spriggan's lungs. A moment later, the spriggan was coughing up the last of the water.

"Are you okay?" Twinket asked her.

"I am now," Kimble said, her voice sounding scratchy and weak. "But I don't think I'll go swimming again any time soon."

"I don't think any of us will," said Kivi.

Aislin noticed that he had his arm around Lin's shoulders. The pedrasi girl didn't seem to mind one bit.

"I'm just glad the horse went after the kelpi," Aislin said, patting the horse's neck. "Poppy, could you please thank him for me?"

"It was Poppy's idea to send the fairy horse after you," Twinket told her.

"Thank you, Poppy," said Aislin. "What made you think of it?"

"When Kimble suddenly disappeared, it occurred to me that there might be kelpi in this lake. My uncle was one of the warriors who helped chase the kelpi out of the land between the mountains," Poppy told her. "He said that the warriors didn't do much. It was really the fairy horses. According to my uncle, fairy horses are the natural enemies of kelpi and go after them every time."

"That's good to know," said Aislin.

"I think we should eat now," said Deela. "Poppy scrounged up nuts and berries. I have a couple of sausages in my bag, and Lin told me that she brought some bread."

"And I have pastries that we can share," said Aislin. "I have hardtack and dried berries, too, but we can save those for when we don't have anything else to eat. Let's eat quickly so we can get back on the road. We were making good headway before we stopped at the lake and I'd like to get as close to the mountain as we can before we stop again."

They started back on the road sooner than Aislin had expected. This time Kimble didn't hide her face in the griffin's feathers. "I almost died, so nothing scares me anymore," she told everyone.

Kivi rode the fairy horse with his arms wrapped around Lin, and they both looked contented. Deela and the manticore seemed to get along well; there was no question that anyone else would ride him.

"I'm sorry I didn't notice the kelpi in the lake," Poppy confessed. "I won't miss anything this time." She turned small in a sparkle of fairy dust and flew ahead of the others.

"I think I'll take a nap," Aislin announced from the crook of Salianne's arm.

"That's a good idea," said Salianne as she strode down the road. "I always say, sleep when you can 'cause you never know when you'll get another chance. No, wait. That's what I say about eating. Well, it's true both ways. Go to sleep, Aislin. I'll keep you safe."

"I'm going to make wreaths out of these dandelions," said Twinket. "Do you want to help me, Tomas?"

"Uh, no thanks," Tomas replied. "I think I'll take a nap, too."

"That's too bad," said Twinket. "You'll be missing out on a lot of fun."

The group moved faster now, eager to put the lake and the kelpies behind them. They passed through the forest as quietly as they could, hurrying when they heard something roar in the distance. Poppy came back a few times to tell them what she had spotted—troll footprints, dragon-blasted trees, and long, coarse fur snagged on twigs too high up to be from a normal animal. Each time she told them of something unusual, they hurried past the spot she'd mentioned, hoping to avoid any more trouble.

No one suggested stopping again until night was falling, but by then they had reached the base of the mountain. A breeze had sprung up, cooling the air, so they knew they'd need a fire to keep warm. They chose a spot far enough from the road that anyone passing by couldn't see the light from the flames. Deela had a way with flint and sticks and soon had a good blaze going. Aislin and Tomas offered to take first watch, having napped for much of the afternoon. After eating the leftovers from their earlier meal, the others lay down close enough to the fire to warm themselves, but far enough that errant sparks wouldn't burn them. When Salianne lay on her side, her body blocked the breeze from reaching her friends.

Aislin and Tomas sat with their backs to the fire so they could see into the darkened forest around them. Although Tomas started at each new or unfamiliar sound, Aislin focused on what the rocks in the ground could tell her. She learned of the smaller animals that scurried about on their own important errands, and the hungry night-prowlers that hunted them. While the fire drew the curious inhabitants of the forest, it repelled others who would normally pass that way. Aislin didn't sense anything dangerous.

After a few hours, Twinket and Kimble's shift began, allowing Aislin and Tomas to lie down near the fire. Neither of the little girls needed much sleep, and they enjoyed staying up to watch the night unfold. Kimble was especially good at seeing in the dark, and was the first to notice the eyes watching them.

"Shh!" she whispered to Twinket. "Don't look now, but someone is in the trees to our left."

"Where?" Twinket asked, turning her head to look.

"I just told you not to look!" Kimble said.

"Then you shouldn't have told me *where* not

to look," Twinket replied. "I wouldn't have known to look there and would have looked somewhere else."

"Shh! There's more of them now," whispered Kimble. "I see at least four sets of eyes reflecting the light from the fire. Some are high and some are low. I think we should wake everyone and tell them."

Twinket got to her feet and started to walk. In a normal voice she said, "I'll wake everyone on this side and you can wake all the others. We can meet in the middle and—"

"What's going on?" Salianne asked, sitting up to look around.

Aislin opened her eyes and peered into the darkness. When she didn't see anything, she reached out with her mind, letting the rocks show her what was near them. There were seven beings out there who didn't feel right. Although some felt human, even they were a little off. Two or three felt partly like animals, and some were almost entirely animals, but the strangest thing was that they all seemed to be changing. Realizing what they must be, she whispered, "They're werewolves."

"Werewolves!" Salianne shouted. "I've never seen werewolves before." She stood up and turned to where the little girls were staring. "I want to catch one and get a good look."

Now that the giantess was no longer lying down, the breeze whipped the fire, making the flames flare and bend while casting bizarre shapes on the surrounding trees. Although Salianne was fourteen feet tall, the shadow she cast made her seem even bigger. As she lumbered toward the trees, there was a yelp and the crack of twigs as the werewolves ran away.

"They're gone now," Aislin told her friends.

Salianne sighed and turned around. "Oh, well," she said. "Maybe next time."

When Tomas gave Aislin a questioning look, she shrugged and whispered, "She's led a very sheltered life and has never ventured beyond a small part of Eliasind. Most of what we've seen today is new to her."

Tomas snorted. "A lot of it is new to me, too."

It took a while before anyone was able to go back to sleep after that, but nothing came near them again.

Chapter 17

AISLIN WOKE EARLY THE next morning. At first she couldn't remember where she was, but when she looked around and saw her friends, she recalled why they were there. She was considering waking everyone so they could all get an early start when she heard the faintest of sounds and felt the presence of fairies. It wasn't just a few fairies, either.

"They're here!" Aislin exclaimed in a voice loud enough to wake everyone but the heaviest sleeper. Grabbing her knapsack that she'd used as a pillow, she ran toward the road.

"Who's here?" Tomas called after her.

She didn't answer as she hurried around trees and over fallen branches. Then her mestari were by her side, watching as a double line of mounted fairies rode from the west with the morning sun glinting off their armor. The fairy horses pranced as if proud to be carrying their riders while the tiny fairies who acted as scouts darted here and there as they reported what they had seen.

"This is really eerie," Tomas whispered to her. "It's an entire army and they don't make a sound. Is there a spell on them?"

Aislin shook her head. "No, fairy horses are always like that when they're in formation. It's one of the things that makes my grandfather's army so effective."

Although the sun was barely up, the light reflecting off the fairies' armor was bright enough to hurt Aislin's eyes. She squinted as the army drew closer. King Darinar rode at the front with Captain Larch beside him. Aislin spotted Sycamore riding behind the captain.

When the king saw his granddaughter, he raised his hand and the army came to a halt. "Hello, my dear. I was wondering when I'd find you," King Darinar said to Aislin. "You shouldn't have come all this way without me. I hope you didn't run into any difficulties."

"Nothing that we couldn't handle," Aislin replied.

"And you have your newest companion with you," he said, and nodded at Salianne. "I worried about you less once Sycamore reported that she had joined your party. He told us about the trolls who attacked you and how Salianne handled them. You were wise to choose her as one of your mestari."

"We're very happy to have her," said Aislin, and flashed a smile at Salianne.

The giantess gazed at the fairy king with her eyes wide and her mouth open. She had never actually met him before, although she had known that he was her friend's grandfather.

"After you left, we located some other fairies who had dealt with Gorinda. They say she was behind much of the unrest," said King Darinar. "What's worse is that she has formed an alliance with the trolls and is controlling them with magic that we haven't seen in a very long time."

"When I visited Mount Gora on behalf of King Talus, I found trolls trying to steal dragon's eggs. They talked about giving them to someone they referred to as 'her,' although they never said who she was or why she wanted the eggs. Do you think it might be Gorinda?"

"Quite possibly," said the king. "If she's stealing

dragons' eggs, I'd like to know where she's taking them and what she has planned. We've been told that she has a stronghold at the top of the mountain. That's where we're going now. I'll have my fairies watch out for dragons' eggs while we're there."

"I can go with you and see if I can learn anything," Aislin suggested. "I can learn a lot when I'm in touch with a mountain."

"No," her grandfather said, shaking his head. "I don't want you anywhere near the fighting. From what we've heard, we'll have to face Gorinda's trolls before we find her. I need to know that you're safe."

Aislin and her party drew back as the army rode past. The princess wasn't expecting Kivi to come up behind her leading the fairy horse. "With your leave, Your Highness, I'll be going now. My place is with the army," the pedrasi warrior said. "I'll come back after the battle to escort you to the palace, but you don't need me now."

"I understand," said Aislin. "Thank you for all you've done."

Aislin's mestari had gathered around her to watch the rest of the columns ride by when the manticore padded up to the princess. "If you don't mind, Bird-brain and I would like to go with the king, too. Baibre told us to help however we can, and we think King Darinar needs us more than you do now."

"Of course, you may go," said Aislin. "I'm sure the king will appreciate your help."

"Ree!" screamed the griffin.

"He says he likes you and wants you to stay safe," the manticore told her.

"I like you both," Aislin told him. "You need to stay safe, too."

"Now what would be the fun in that?" the manticore asked, then turned and bounded away.

Deela joined Aislin as the manticore fell in line behind the mounted warriors while the griffin circled over the columns. "Be careful, Snick!" the orc girl called after the manticore.

"Is that his name?" Aislin asked her. "I never heard it before."

"The griffin had a name, but the manticore didn't, so I gave him one," said Deela. "I named him after my cousin. They have the same eyes."

"If we have to stay here, I'm going to look for were-wolf tracks," said Salianne. "Anyone want to join me?"

"I will," Lin said.

"I'm going, too," Kimble announced. "I want to see what you do when you actually catch a werewolf."

While the trio went off to scour the forest floor for tracks, Aislin and Tomas returned to the campfire to douse the ashes with water. As they were finishing up, they heard a shout and Lin came running back.

"Come see what we found!" Lin cried.

"Did you find werewolf tracks?" asked Tomas.

"No, something even better," said Lin. "We found Aghamonda's tracks and they lead right into the mountain!"

"I want to see this," Aislin said. "If Aghamonda is heading into the mountain, she might be planning to help Gorinda."

With Lin in the lead, Aislin, Tomas, and the rest of her ladies hurried through the forest, watching for more tracks. They found them in the soil at the base of the scree and again on the slope where Salianne and Kimble were waiting. Although they looked like the footprints of any full-sized fairy, the impression they made in the soil was much deeper. Whoever had walked there weighed a lot more than an ordinary fairy. "I think they're at least half a day old," Lin told them. "See over there. They head right into that opening." The young pedrasi showed them a gap in the side of the mountain that was big enough for two full-sized fairies or one ordinary orc.

"Then that's where I need to go," Aislin said, and turned to her companions. "I'm going in, but that doesn't mean you have to. Salianne, you'll have to stay out here because you won't fit. Besides, I need someone to make sure that no one follows us inside. And anyone who is afraid of the dark or confined spaces should stay out here, too. I don't want someone panicking when we're in the mountain."

"Give me a minute and I can make everyone fairy lights," said Poppy. "Do you have yours with you, Aislin?"

"I don't," Aislin replied. "I lost it in Mount Gora."

While Poppy started forming fairy lights with her hands, Aislin turned to the others.

"You know I'm used to the dark and small spaces," Lin told her. "I grew up inside Deephold."

"And I grew up in Mount Gora," said Kimble. "I'm going in."

"I'm fine with the dark and small spaces," said Tomas. "I'm going in."

"So am I," Deela told them. "I spent the first ten years of my life inside a mountain without ever seeing the light of day. Why do you think you never see little orcs running around? We're not allowed outside until we graduate from basic warrior training and can take care of ourselves."

"Twinket, that leaves you," Aislin said, turning to the doll. "Would you mind staying out here to keep watch with Salianne? It would help me a lot if you did."

"Oh no, you're not tricking me like that. If you're going in, so am I!" Twinket replied.

"Are you sure?" Aislin asked her. "You told me how much you hate being closed up in anything small like a satchel. If we find ourselves in a tight space or lose our lights for some reason, you might be terrified."

"I'll be even more terrified if I have to stay outside not knowing what's happening to you," said Twinket. "I'm going in whether you want me there or not!"

Chapter 18

THE DISTANT ROAR OF attacking trolls and the cries of their victims made everyone look up. The sound was coming from so high on the mountain that they couldn't see anything.

"The battle between the fairies and the trolls must have started," Aislin remarked. "If we can't help up there, at least we can see what Aghamonda is doing and stop her from joining the battle."

Poppy handed out the apple-sized fairy lights she had made, giving Salianne one as well. The sunlight was so bright that the glow from the lights seemed pale and wan in comparison. "I saw the way you were looking at the lights. It won't do you much good until it gets dark, but it's yours to keep for later," Poppy told the giant.

"Where'd it go?" Salianne said, unable to find it in her hand.

"It fell down between your fingers," said Twinket. "Let me get it."

The giantess set her hand on the ground, letting Twinket climb up. When the doll reached between Salianne's fingers, her little arms disappeared up to her elbows. "Found it!" she finally said, showing the fairy light to everyone.

"Take care of yourself," Aislin told Salianne, then turned to the mountain. With Tomas right behind her, the rest of Aislin's mestari followed single-file through the opening.

They had walked only a few yards when Kimble pushed past Tomas so she could be closer to Aislin. The little spriggan reached up to tug on the hem of Aislin's tunic. "I can be your scout," Kimble told her.

"Not until I have an idea of what we might expect," Aislin replied.

The opening was the start of a long and narrow tunnel. Enough light came in from the outside that they could see for a dozen yards in, but then the tunnel changed direction, cutting off the light. It would have been completely dark if not for the fairy lights that gave off a warm glow and lit up the space around them. Suddenly everyone appreciated Poppy's fairy lights. They started playing with them, waving their hands to direct the lights back and forth in front of them.

"Please stop that!" Aislin said when Kimble's light bumped the back of her head the second time and Twinket's light made swirly patterns before her eyes.

"Don't you need a light, Poppy?" asked Lin, who was in line right behind the fairy.

"No, I'll be fine," Poppy replied. A moment later she turned tiny and rose into the air.

"Ooh!" said Deela when the beating of Poppy's wings created a soft light. "I never get tired of seeing that."

"Hold on a minute," Aislin announced. "Let me find out what we're getting into." Placing her hand on the wall, she closed her eyes and reached out with her mind. She could feel the tunnel extend deep into the mountain with other tunnels intersecting it here and there. Although the tunnel they were in seemed safe enough at first, she could sense a deep pit only a few hundred feet ahead, and rocks balanced past that to fall on anyone agile enough to jump over the pit. Extending her search, she found tunnels that were safe for a time, but led to deep ravines or narrowed down to spaces so small that people could get trapped inside.

Twinket and Kimble started fidgeting behind her and the noise began to pull her away from her search. "Shh," Lin whispered. "She's busy. You have to be quiet."

Aislin reached farther out then, searching the mountain for the presence of anything unusual. She located Aghamonda, standing inside a tunnel that didn't look promising at first. When Aislin felt past the fairy statue, she found a heavy stone door and a descending tunnel behind it. Curious, the princess traced it to a lower level, then another until she reached a level with an enormous cavern. A lake three times the size of the one in Mount Gora took up most of the cavern floor, while cracks in the floor around the lake allowed steam to escape from below. A narrow bridge connected the shore to a stone platform that stood on pillars in the very center of the lake.

Although it wasn't easy, Aislin tried to get a

feeling for what was on the platform. There were trolls there and something she couldn't quite make out. When she focused, she could almost sense…Suddenly a red-hot light seemed to pierce her mind and she lurched back into herself so fast that she gasped.

"What is it?" asked Tomas. "What did you see?"

"I think I saw the sorceress," Aislin told him. "But she isn't on the top of the mountain. She's two levels down in the middle of a lake with lots and lots of trolls."

"We should go tell your grandfather," said Tomas.

Aislin nodded. "Someone certainly should. Poppy, would you mind going? You can find him faster than anyone."

Poppy darted up to hover beside the princess. "I'll do whatever you need, Aislin. But what are you going to do?"

"Talk to Aghamonda and find out what's going on," the princess told her. "Now hurry, my grandfather needs to know where the sorceress really is."

Aislin started walking again the moment Poppy left. The princess headed to the next tunnel, which was safe enough for a short distance.

"Stay to the left," she told the others as they approached a sheer drop.

"Duck and make sure you don't touch the rock hanging down in the middle," she warned as they neared a precariously balanced boulder.

They had reached the entrance to another tunnel where Aislin was about to turn when Kimble sent her light bobbing straight down the tunnel they were in. "I can look ahead if you want me to," the spriggan said as she edged past Aislin. "This part looks fine to me."

Kimble ran ahead before Aislin could stop her. Skidding on a particularly smooth spot, the little spriggan turned to look back.

"I'm going, too!" Twinket cried, and tried to inch past Aislin.

"Don't move!" Aislin told her, holding out her hand. "Twinket, get behind me. Kimble, the floor under your feet is very, very thin. It didn't break because you don't weigh much, but if you stomp your feet or anyone else steps on it, it will break and you'll fall a very long way. Now, slide your feet without lifting them and come back to me."

Kimble's eyes went wide and she looked from side to side without moving her head. "I just wanted to help," she said, sounding shaky.

"I know you did," Aislin said.

Crack! The tiny sound made Kimble jerk. Suddenly cracks spiderwebbed under her little feet, spreading across the smooth rock. Aislin closed her eyes and set her hand on the wall. She centered herself and felt the cracks opening wider. Reaching into the rock, she filled in the cracks, pulling strength from the rock walls.

It was hard for Aislin to focus on what she was doing and to talk at the same time. When she said, "Now run!" her voice sounded strained.

Kimble ran then, with the cracks reappearing with each step. When she was close enough, she jumped into Aislin's arms. "Do not go in front of me again," the princess ordered as she set Kimble down.

"I won't, I swear!" the spriggan exclaimed.

"Kimble and Twinket can walk with me while you concentrate on what lies ahead," said Lin.

The mestari followed Aislin into the other tunnel. When they reached a spot where the passage narrowed, Aislin noticed that the floor was covered with thin bits of shattered stone. Feeling the passage with her senses, she discovered that the ceiling was covered with sharp needles of stone that would fall at the smallest vibration. Anyone walking under them wouldn't stand a chance. Wondering why she hadn't noticed the needles in her first search, she began to examine the tunnels even more closely.

"This is taking too long," Kimble whined.

"Sorry," Aislin replied. "But we just passed three traps and a pit that appears to be bottomless. I'd rather be slow and careful than fast and lose someone."

"I know my senses aren't as strong as yours, but the tunnel that goes off to the right about ten feet ahead might be safer than the others," said Lin.

Aislin nodded. "I think it is. I also think that's the one the sorceress uses."

"Finally!" Deela muttered. "My neck is killing me from ducking all the time."

"Just so you know, Aghamonda is in this tunnel," Aislin warned them. "We have to get past her before we can continue on."

"Then Deela and I should go first," Lin said, trying to push past Tomas.

"Not now," said Aislin. "I can handle a statue."

Waving at her fairy light, she sent it into the tunnel. She followed it, already looking for Aghamonda. When she didn't see the statue, she searched with her mind and found it behind an outcropping only yards away.

"I know where you are," Aislin called out. "What are you doing here?"

"Waiting for you," Aghamonda said as she stepped into view. "I knew you'd follow me, especially after I left such obvious footprints."

"Why are you working for Gorinda?"

"I'm not working *for* anyone," said Aghamonda. "I'm working *with* her."

"And was it your idea for you to stand here in the dark or did she order you to?" asked Aislin.

"She asked me to, very nicely," Aghamonda replied.

"What does Gorinda want anyway? Why is she doing all this?"

"Ask her yourself, if you can get past me."

"Of course I can get past you," Aislin replied. "You're a statue and you have no magic." Drawing strength from the mountain itself, the princess pulled power into her voice when she said, "Step aside and let us pass."

The statue staggered a few steps, then stopped and swayed back and forth as if struggling to keep still. "You...can't...make—" she choked out.

This time Aislin closed her eyes. The battle was already engaged on the mountainside, so she didn't have time to waste. If controlling the person who was the statue didn't work, perhaps she should go straight to the stone. Drawing more power into herself, she sent it into the statue, shifting it here, pushing it there so that it moved back behind the outcropping and froze in place. "Now don't move until the fairy king sends for you," Aislin added, making the feet of the statue meld with the rock floor and its hands adhere to its hips.

"You can't do this!" Aghamonda shouted. "Gorinda won't be happy."

"I'm not here to make her happy," Aislin said, then turned back to her friends. "You can come through now."

"If it isn't the prince!" Aghamonda said as Tomas passed by. "I should have known you'd be with her."

"Still in trouble, huh, Aghamonda?" said Tomas.

"Always!" she replied with a smirk, as if it was a good thing.

When Kimble, Lin, and Deela walked by, she told them, "That princess is leading you to your doom. Run away while you can."

Kimble stuck her tongue out at Aghamonda. With a wave of her hand, the little spriggan made her fairy light bounce off the statue's nose. Aghamonda didn't seem to notice. "That statue is as dumb as a box of rocks," Kimble told her companions as they hurried on. "I'd never trust a blockhead like her!"

The tunnel opened into a slightly wider passage. While Aislin paused to "see" what lay ahead, Lin led the way. "There's a stone door blocking the tunnel," the pedrasi girl said. "I'll open it."

Aghamonda laughed while Lin tried to lift the latch. She tried harder, pushing with both hands until her face turned red. The harder Lin tried, the more Aghamonda laughed. When the latch still didn't budge, the pedrasi finally resorted to tapping it with her war hammer, but even that didn't work.

"Maybe if I help you . . ." said Deela.

They both tried then, but nothing happened. Aghamonda roared with laughter.

"Why are you laughing?" Tomas asked the statue.

"Because they'll never get that door open, no matter how strong they are," Aghamonda replied. "Gorinda put a spell on it so I'm the only one who can open it. Nothing that lives and breathes can open that door, but I can as long as I'm a statue. And don't bother asking—you'll never get me to open it for you."

"We don't need to ask you," said Twinket. "If you can do it, I can, too. I'm not actually alive and I don't breathe."

While Lin and Deela backed away, the little doll strode to the door, tilting her head back to see the latch high above her. "Uh, can someone pick me up?" she asked. "I can't reach that latch."

"Here you go," Deela said, picking up Twinket.

When the orc held Twinket up to the latch, the doll put both of her soft, cloth hands on it and pushed. The door groaned open, letting a draft of cool, damp air waft through the tunnel. Twinket grinned and clapped her hands. "Now aren't you glad I came?" she asked the others.

"Aislin, are you ready?" Tomas asked.

The princess had been aware of everything that was going on around her even as she cast her senses into the depths of the mountain. She had heard what Aghamonda had said about opening the door. Aislin knew that she could have moved the wall itself if necessary, but she was glad that Twinket had figured it out and was so happy about it.

Opening her eyes, Aislin blinked and said, "I am. I was trying to see how many trolls are with Gorinda, but there are too many to count."

"That doesn't sound good," Tomas said, shaking his head.

Once again Aislin led the way. Although she kept *feeling* what lay ahead, she didn't discover any more traps. They descended two more levels. As they neared the cavern, they began to hear the grumbling of trolls and smelled something unpleasant.

"I smell trolls and sulfur," said Deela.

Kimble took one sniff and shuddered. Pinching her nose shut, she said, "I smell rotten eggs and stinky feet."

The noise and the stench grew stronger as the party headed down the sloping tunnel. They weren't far from the tunnel's end when wisps of fog began to curl around them. The fog grew thicker until they entered the cavern itself. Although Aislin could sense the cavern floor, the air was so filled with moisture that their fairy lights were just small patches of not-quite-so-dark mist. When she took a few steps, the air seemed a bit clearer. "Come on," she said, and her friends crowded behind her, bumping into her as she moved forward ever so slowly.

"What's down here?" Deela asked as a breath of air moved past them, making the fog thin and thicken.

"There's a lake straight ahead about twenty feet," replied Aislin. "Watch out for trolls and the sorceress. And tell me if you see anything else that's unusual."

"Like that?" Lin asked, pointing at something glowing in the fog only yards away.

A few steps took them close enough to see a stone vent in the ground releasing steam into the air. Lin was closer to the vent than the others when she said, "Ow! I kicked something," and bent down to look at the bumpy, foot-long objects.

"Are those dragon eggs?" asked Tomas as he reached out to touch one.

"They are," Aislin said. "The trolls must have been stealing them from other mountains and not just Mount Gora. This must be where they're bringing them. I'll have to tell my grandfather."

There was a louder roar from the trolls and everyone in Aislin's party turned toward the lake. The air was clearer there with a light breeze blowing the fog away. Aislin could see the platform easily now. Flaming torches ringed it on all sides. In the center of the platform, the floor was raised and someone had erected four ornate columns to hold up a simple peaked roof. More trolls than Aislin had ever seen before milled around on the platform, although they avoided the center. The only one on the raised part of the platform was a figure wearing a black cape. The hood of the cape was thrown back, exposing the long scarlet hair and delicate features of a woman. She stood with her head bowed, gazing down into the lake.

"That must be the sorceress!" Aislin told her friends.

"Look at the lake," Tomas said, and they all stepped closer. The water was perfectly smooth without a ripple on its surface.

"Wow!" Aislin exclaimed. Inches below the surface of the water the image of the mountaintop was clearly visible. Clouds scudded past it, obscuring then revealing the mounted fairies battling a horde of trolls carrying clubs and axes. Her grandfather was there in the thick of the fighting, along with Sycamore and Kivi. Wielding magic as skillfully as he wielded his sword, the fairy king hurled bolts of power at his enemies while his warriors used magic blades to cut down the trolls and the manticore and griffin attacked with teeth and claws.

At first Aislin thought that the fairies were winning, but she soon realized that whenever a troll fell three more ran to take its place even if they hadn't seen their companion struck down. Aislin wondered how they knew to do this when she glanced up and saw the hooded figure waving her arms as if she was a general directing her troops. "She's telling the trolls what to do from down here where she's safe," said Aislin.

She was turning her head when she glimpsed something moving near the tunnel entrance. It was a tiny fairy, appearing and disappearing as she flew through the patchy fog. When Aislin could see her well enough, she recognized Hydrangea.

The fairy was obviously agitated when she reached Gorinda. The sorceress watched her dart back and forth in front of her for a few moments before screaming, "Quiet! I can't hear a thing she says!" over the racket that the trolls were making.

The sudden silence was almost shocking.

Everyone watched Hydrangea turn big in front of Gorinda. The sorceress shook her head as the fairy gestured with her hands. "Who did what to Aghamonda?" Gorinda shouted loud enough for everyone to hear. "Of course, she's still a statue. That's because of your incompetence! Who did she say is here?"

The sorceress paused for a few seconds as she listened to the fairy, then shouted, "Oh, really?"

"Is she talking about us?" Kimble whispered.

"Shhh!" Lin told her, even as the sorceress turned to the trolls.

"That princess you were supposed to bring to me is here now," Gorinda yelled. "Find her!" With one wave of her arms, the fog disappeared, leaving Aislin and her friends in clear sight.

The princess looked at the vents and the rock walls. There was nowhere to hide, the trolls had already spotted them, and the tunnel entrance was too far away to reach now. "Don't fight," Aislin told her friends as the trolls came thundering across the bridge and around the lake. "Put your weapons away until I tell you to take them out again."

"But Your Highness," Deela began.

"There are too many trolls," said Aislin. "Let them take us to her. Don't resist or they're more likely to hurt you."

Deela and Lin looked grim, but it was Tomas who said, "I don't like this."

"I know," Aislin told him, and reached out to squeeze his arm.

"Just throw up a wall like you did in Mount Gora," said Kimble. "If you block them in I can jump on them from behind and snick-snack," she said, making thrusting movements with her knife. "Then I'm on to the next one."

"We're not fighting them, Kimble," said Aislin. "At least not yet. I need to deal with Gorinda now and end the fighting on the mountaintop. Just trust that I know what I'm doing."

The little spriggan's mouth snapped shut. Although she looked angry, she didn't say another word as she put her knife away. The trolls were on them in seconds.

Armed with clubs and axes, the snarling, growling trolls surrounded them. Up close, the reek of so many trolls made Aislin's eyes water.

"Fight!" one shouted.

"We want fight you!" shouted another.

"We're not going to fight you, so just take us to Gorinda," Aislin told them.

One of the trolls shoved Tomas with a club. Another took a swipe at Deela, barely missing her. The trolls looked disgusted when neither one responded. "You no fun!" a troll grumbled.

Aislin really didn't want her mestari to fight the trolls yet, and she was proud of them for holding back, but she promised herself that it wouldn't be for long.

The trolls hustled them across the narrow stone bridge, but didn't follow the princess and her friends onto the raised part of the platform. Aislin saw Gorinda waiting for them just ahead with Hydrangea hovering above her. Up close, the sorceress was pretty, with bright red hair that hung loose in waves down the sides of her face. Her lips were the same shade of red and her eyes were so dark that they nearly looked black. Aislin thought she looked familiar, though she knew she had never seen her before.

"I know who you are, so don't pretend that you aren't you," Gorinda yelled as Aislin stepped onto the raised platform. "My spies have told me everything about Princess Aislin! I've been trying to get my incompetent helpers to bring you to me, but they're all nitwits who don't know their elbows from their eyeballs. And then you showed up all on your own. Thank you for that—you saved me a whole lot of trouble."

From what she could see of Hydrangea, Aislin thought the tiny fairy looked smug.

"Why do you want me?" asked Aislin.

"Speak up!" The sorceress shouted. "I hate mumblers. I've been lightning-struck too many times, and I can't hear a ding-dong thing unless you talk louder."

"I said, 'Why do you want me?'" Aislin yelled.

"Because I hate your grandparents! They stole the throne from me and locked me away in an ice cave. I only just got out." The sorceress shivered and pulled her cape closer around herself. "I've been cold for so long and now I can't get warm no matter what I do."

"You still didn't answer my question," Aislin shouted. "Why are you after me?"

"I've spent years trying to think of ways to get back at King Darinar and Queen Surinen. When I heard that they had a granddaughter they were crazy about, I said to myself, what better way to get back at them than to hurt the one they adore? I just wish I could see the looks on their faces when they hear what I've done to you. Hey, maybe I could use a spell to spy on them so I can see it. That's a great idea! And then I can—"

"What about the dragon eggs? Why are you collecting them?" shouted Aislin.

"Who needs fairy horses when you have dragons? With them in my army, I'll be invincible. Besides,

dragons are the best fire starters I know. I need something to warm my fingers and toes." Thrusting her
arms out from under her cape, she held up her mit-
tened hands.

"You can't keep the princess here," Hydrangea
shouted at Gorinda. "What are you going to do with
her?"

The sorceress gave Aislin an appraising look, then
yelled to the trolls, "Take the princess and her friends
away. Dispose of them however you want to, but make
sure you bring back Aislin's royal head so I can send it
to King Darinar and Queen Surinen."

The trolls grinned and started toward Aislin and
her mestari, but the princess was ready. The entire
time Aislin had been listening to Gorinda, she had
been drawing power from the rock platform into herself. The trolls were only a few feet away when Aislin
gestured. The cavern trembled as the end of the platform rose up, creating a wall in front of the trolls.

"What the—" cried Gorinda. "How did you do
that? I don't know of any magic that can control
rock that way. Hold on. Now it's my turn." Raising her
hands, she twirled them around, then made a sweeping motion at the water. A wave rose up from the lake

and slammed into the platform. Before it could wash her friends away, Aislin created another wall to block it. The wave crashed into the new wall, sending spray high into the air and drenching Gorinda. Hydrangea darted out of the way and fled to the tunnel.

While Gorinda spluttered and shivered, Aislin reached into her knapsack and pulled out the calcite globe. Bending down, she whispered to Kimble, "Jinxie told me about Old Grumpy. Was everything he said true?"

"It sure was," said Kimble.

Aislin straightened up and turned to the lake. Pulling back her arm, she threw the globe at the very edge of the platform, smashing the calcite into a dozen pieces. The globe and its contents fell into the water, disappearing into the depths.

"Now you can fight," she told her companions. "Push as many trolls as you can into the water, but make sure you don't fall in, too." With another gesture, she removed the wall, making it sink back into the platform to become part of the floor.

Surprised, the trolls weren't expecting Deela, Lin, and Tomas to fall on them with sword and hammer. Kimble went after the nearest troll, slicing at its hairy, knobby legs with her knife while Twinket darted between the combatants, jabbing the trolls' feet and ankles with her pins. Within the first minute, three trolls fell into the lake where they splashed around and tried to climb atop one another to escape the water.

Suddenly one of the trolls screamed, "Something nibbling me!" His screams grew louder until he disappeared with a *whoosh*.

Soon a second troll was screaming, too. "Something chomping me!" he cried before disappearing under the water.

The third troll didn't have time to scream more than "Help!" before something dragged him under.

After the last troll disappeared, Aislin glanced into the water. She could see the shape of something large and pale that seemed to be growing even as she watched. As the fighting continued and more trolls fell in, the creature grew until it was massive. The fighting became fiercer as the trolls saw what had happened to their friends. Tomas was grappling with a troll when it slipped and started to fall. Deela had to grab Tomas and jerk him back when he almost fell in as well.

"We have to get to the shore," Aislin told Lin.

The pedrasi girl nodded and told the others even as she hacked a path through the trolls. When the creature leapt out of the water to grab the trolls closest to the edge, Lin saw her opportunity and urged her friends to cross over the bridge. Twinket was trying to poke the back of a troll's leg and didn't see Lin, so Deela scooped up the doll and ran with her. Most of the trolls were watching their friends disappear and didn't see when Aislin's party ran past them. Two trolls ran into the tunnel, screaming. Seeing them flee, the rest of the trolls ran after them, shrieking so loudly that the sound hurt Aislin's ears.

Aislin and her group were near the cavern wall when the princess turned back to look for Gorinda. The sorceress was the only one on the platform and she was furious. Although she must have lost sight of Aislin when the trolls were fleeing, she saw her now. Screaming, "I hate you! You spoiled everything!" the sorceress began waving her arms and pointing at Aislin.

As waves rose up and crashed over the shore, Aislin drew more power from the rock around her. Closing her eyes, she reached out to open fault lines and weaken the stone near Gorinda. Ever so slowly, the platform began to tilt. Suddenly the columns collapsed, the roof slid into the lake and the entire platform tilted onto its side. Deela grabbed Aislin just before Gorinda's wave hit. Holding the princess with one arm and a rock outcropping with another, the orc took the brunt of the wave's force.

Gorinda screamed, but instead of tumbling into the water, she seemed to hang motionless as silver sparkles surrounded her. Aislin gasped when Gorinda turned into a tiny fairy and darted out of the tunnel. "Did you see that?" the princess asked her friends.

"I did," said Tomas, but he was staring at the creature in the lake and not at the tunnel. The creature was finishing off the trolls that had fallen in and looked as if it was at least a hundred feet long. "And I think it's time to go before that thing figures out how to get out of the water."

Chapter 19

SALIANNE HAD JUST REJOINED Aislin, Tomas, and the rest of the mestari when King Darinar and his army rode down the side of the mountain looking battle-worn but happy. "The trolls stopped fighting suddenly and fled the mountainside. I assume that had something to do with you," the king said as he stopped his fairy horse beside the princess.

"Gorinda left," she said. "But I think she lost control of her army before that."

King Darinar listened closely as Aislin told him everything that had happened. When she finished her story and said, "So she really is a fairy," the king nodded.

"I knew there was something familiar about her," said Aislin. "She had fairy features and was beautiful like a fairy."

"Your grandmother and I suspected who she was," King Darinar told her. "The sorceress was using ancient spells that no one uses anymore, although it makes sense if she had remained in the ice cave all those years. Your description of her confirms our suspicions. Her real name is Firethorn and she was a powerful and most unpleasant fairy. Although she never did sit on the throne, she did try to take over the fairy world once a long time ago. If she'd had her way, she would have destroyed everything so she could rebuild it the way she wanted. She started by infesting a forest with firethorns. Your grandmother and I had to weed her out before she could do any more damage. Lightning was one of the few things that worked on her."

"If she was so powerful, why didn't she try to use other spells on us?" asked Aislin. "Firethorn created waves and sent her trolls after us, but I would have expected more from a powerful fairy."

"Fairy magic comes from living things and sunlight," the king replied. "You were deep in a mountain where sunlight cannot reach. Firethorn may have chosen that cavern because fairies couldn't do much to her there, but then she wasn't expecting magic like yours. I doubt her spies knew what you could do, or they would have told her."

"Do you think she's gone for good?" asked Aislin.

King Darinar shook his head. "I doubt that very much. The real question is, where will she turn up next?" She's always been stubborn and persistent. She's also exceedingly hard to defeat. The fact that you defeated her in battle is amazing. No one else could have done what you did."

"I couldn't have done it without my mestari," said Aislin. "Poppy has her magic, knows things about fairies that I don't, and is a messenger I can trust. Lin and Deela can take down trolls single-handed and are the only guards I need. Kimble is clever, fierce, and deadly. Salianne can throw trolls great distances and scare away werewolves just by standing up. And Twinket can open doors and fit into spaces that others can't. When we were in Morain, I learned that she also makes an excellent spy. I'm very proud of my mestari and think they're perfect for the job."

"You *should* be proud of all your mestari," King

Darinar told her. "Your grandmother and I believe that you made excellent choices. When we get back to Fairengar, we'll hold a banquet to honor all of you. Soon everyone will know that your mestari are just what a princess like you needs."